Features to look out for...

Throughout this sample chapter, you'll get a glimpse of all the features that will help your students succeed in history.

Key Term
Unfamiliar and historically important words are defined for students.

Exam-style questions
Realistic exam-style questions appear in every chapter with short tips to help students get started with their answers – ideal for homework and assessments.

1.1 Anglo-Saxon society

Extend your knowledge

Thegns
Thegns were divided into king's thegns, who held their land direct from the king and served him directly, and those who held their land from earls and other thegns.

When a man became a thegn, he paid a tax called a heriot. Heriot meant 'war gear' and the tax required a thegn to equip himself with a helmet and coat of mail, a horse and harness, and a sword and spear.

Earls
Earls* were the most important aristocrats: the most important men in the country after the king. The relationship between the king and his earls was based on loyalty. The earls competed against each other to be the one the king trusted and relied on the most, so that the king would give them the greatest rewards and honour. Sometimes, earls even challenged the king to get more power.

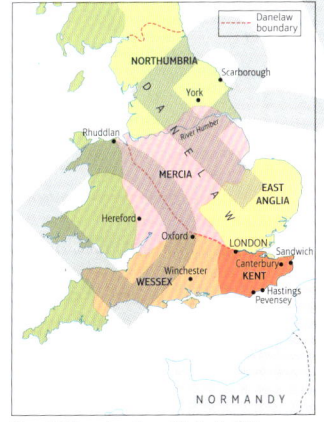

Figure 1.2 The main earldoms of England in 1060.

Key term

Earls*
Highest Anglo-Saxon aristocracy. The word came from the Danish 'jarl' and meant a chieftain who ruled a region on behalf of the king. The area controlled by an earl is called an earldom.

Changing social status
In other parts of Europe, such as in Normandy, people's status in society depended on ancestry: the importance of their family and ancestors. Anglo-Saxon society was much less rigid than this.

- A peasant who prospered and obtained five hides of land that he paid tax on could gain the status of a thegn.
- Merchants who made a number of trips abroad in their own ships could also become thegns.
- Slaves could be freed by their masters – and free peasants could sell themselves into slavery as a desperate measure to feed their families.
- At the top of the social system, thegns could be raised to the status of earls (and earls could be demoted to thegns). Earls could sometimes even become kings.

Exam-style question, Section B
Describe **two** features of the social system of Anglo-Saxon England. **4 marks**

Exam tip
This question is about identifying key features. You need to identify two relevant points and then develop each point. For example: 'The social system was not fixed. This meant a free peasant who did very well could become a thegn.'

Extend your knowledge

Anglo-Saxon England
The areas of Britain controlled by Anglo-Saxons had changed over the centuries. Viking invasions had taken control of vast areas, which had then been recaptured. Anglo-Saxon England also had hostile neighbours: Wales, Scotland and Ireland and, to the south, Normandy. The location of Normandy is included on this map, but it was never under Anglo-Saxon control.

The power of the English monarchy
In 1060, the king (monarch) was Edward the Confessor. He was the most powerful person in Anglo-Saxon England. He governed the country.

Powers of the king
- **Law-making:** the king created new laws and made sure they were enforced throughout the country.
- **Money:** the king controlled the production of the silver pennies used as money.
- **Landownership:** the king owned large estates and could grant land out to his followers. He could also take land away from those who had acted against him.
- **Military power:** the king had the ability to raise a national army and fleet.
- **Taxation:** the king decided when taxes should be paid and a national taxation system delivered this tax to him.

Duties of the people
- To obey the law as it was passed down through the king's local representatives.
- To use the king's coins. Forging coins was a very serious crime.
- Land carried with it obligations to the king. The main two obligations were payment of tax and military service.
- Landholders had to provide and equip fighters for the army or fleet; otherwise they were fined or lost their land.
- Landholders had to pay their taxes, otherwise they were fined or lost their land.

Figure 1.3 The powers of Edward the Confessor and the duties of his people. The image in the middle is a representation of Edward's royal seal. This was attached to his royal orders to show they came from the king.

The king's role was to protect his people from attack and give them laws to maintain safety and security at home. In return, the people of England owed him service. Every boy swore an oath* when they reached 12 years of age to be faithful to the king. The oath was administered by the shire reeve* at a special ceremony held each year (see Source A).

Source A
The oath sworn by Anglo-Saxon boys once they reached 12 years of age.

All shall swear in the name of the Lord, before whom every holy thing is holy, that they will be faithful to the king... From the day on which this oath shall be rendered, no one shall conceal the breach of it on the part of a brother or family relation, any more than in a stranger.

How powerful was Edward the Confessor?
Kings of Anglo-Saxon England held their power ultimately because they led armies. Anglo-Saxon kings had clawed England back from Viking control. Edward the Confessor was not a warrior king, but his earls and their thegns were a powerful military force and he relied on his earls, especially Earl Godwin, to protect England from attack.

Kings who were war leaders gained legitimacy for their rule because they could hand out the wealth and land of their defeated enemies to their followers. When kings did not have success in battle then their power could be reduced. However, Edward had other reasons that made him a legitimate king.

Key terms

Oath*
A solemn promise to do something. Anglo-Saxons swore oaths on holy relics to make them especially binding. A relic was often a body part of a dead saint, kept in a special casket.

Shire reeve*
An official of the king: his sheriff. Sheriffs managed the king's estates, collected revenue for him and were in charge of local courts.

Extend your knowledge
Extra details to deepen students' knowledge and understanding.

Sources
A wide variety of contemporary sources help bring the subject to life, and give important insight into each period.

Features to look out for...

1.2 The last years of Edward the Confessor and the succession crisis

Source B
The death of Edward the Confessor, portrayed in the Bayeux Tapestry.

Activity
KWL is a strategy to help you take control of your own learning. It stands for Know – Want to know – Learned. This is how it works:

a   Draw a table with three columns: 'Know', 'Want to know', 'Learned'.
b   For any topic you are learning about, write down what you know about it already.
c   Next, write down what else you'd like know, what questions you have about what you know.
d   When you find out the answers, write them in the 'Learned' column.

Use this method to make notes on this section. Here's an example:

Know	Want to know	Learned
Tostig was from Wessex; Northumbria was different.	Why was Northumbria different?	Part of Northumbria in Danelaw. Different laws, different language, tax lower.

Summary
- The house of Godwin had become the real 'power behind the throne' in Anglo-Saxon England.
- Harold's embassy to Normandy and his decisions over Tostig had major consequences.
- Edward the Confessor died childless, causing a succession crisis.

Checkpoint
Strengthen
S1 When did: Harold become Earl of Wessex; Tostig get exiled; King Edward die?
S2 Describe two aspects of the house of Godwin that made them so powerful.

Challenge
C1 In your own words, summarise three reasons why you think Harold went against King Edward's wishes over the rising against Tostig.
C2 What else would it be useful to know about the consequences of Tostig's exile?

How confident do you feel about your answers to these questions? If you are not sure that you have answered them well, try the above study skills activity.

Activities
Engaging and accessible activities tailored to the skills focuses of each unit to support and stretch students' learning.

Summary
Bullet-point list of the key points from the material at the end of each chunk of learning – great for embedding the core knowledge and handy for revision.

Checkpoint
Students are asked to check and reflect on their learning regularly.

'**Strengthen**' sections help consolidate knowledge and understanding.

'**Challenge**' questions encourage evaluation and analysis of what's being studied.

At the end of each chapter, '**Recap**' spreads give students a chance to consolidate and reflect upon what they've learned. These sections include a recall quiz (ideal for a quick-fire knowledge check in class or revision aid), activities to help students summarise and analyse the chapter, and consider how it links to what they've learned throughout the course.

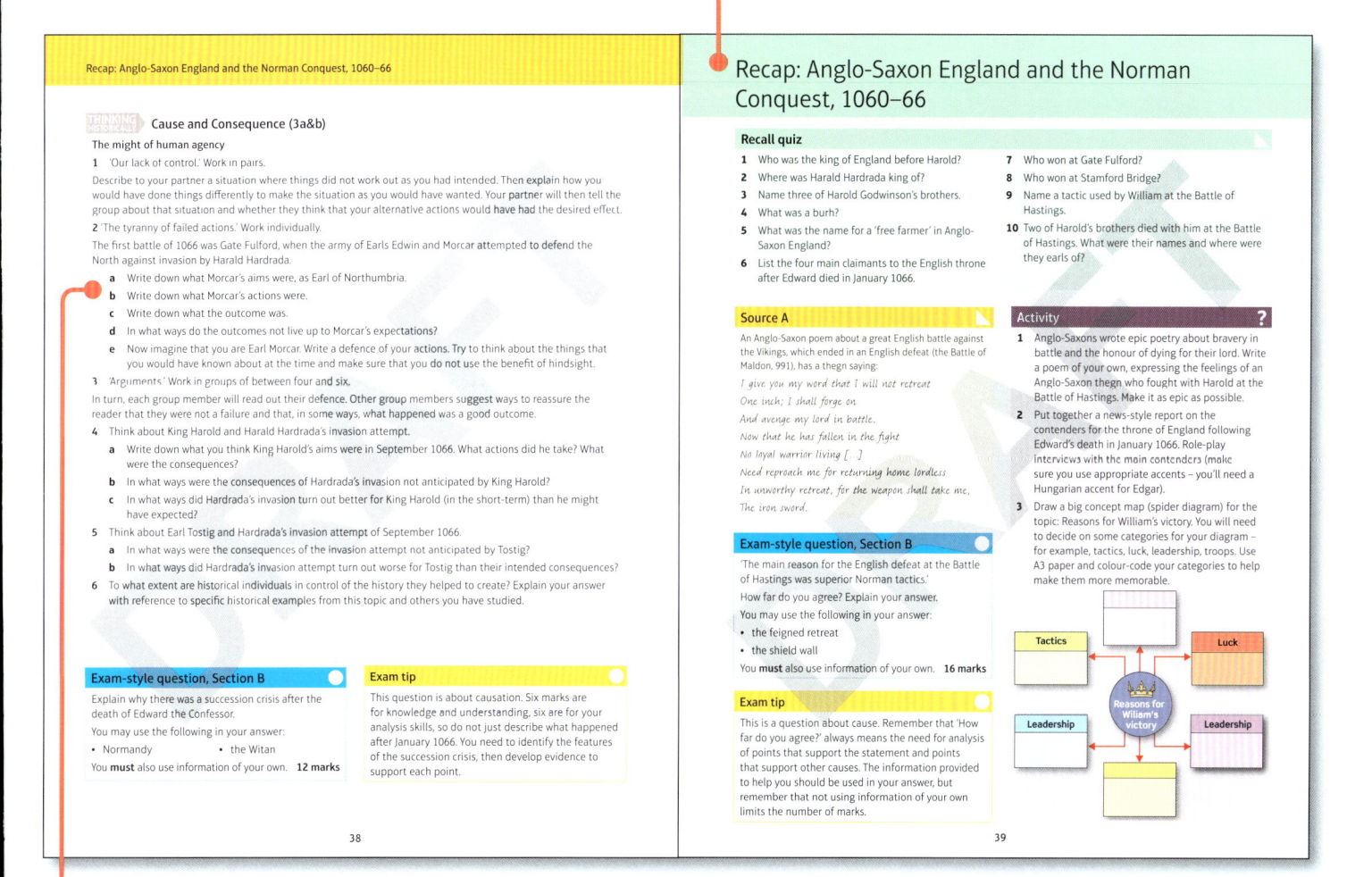

Recap: Anglo-Saxon England and the Norman Conquest, 1060–66

Cause and Consequence (3a&b)

The might of human agency

1 'Our lack of control.' Work in pairs.
Describe to your partner a situation where things did not work out as you had intended. Then explain how you would have done things differently to make the situation as you would have wanted. Your partner will then tell the group about that situation and whether they think that your alternative actions would have had the desired effect.

2 'The tyranny of failed actions.' Work individually.
The first battle of 1066 was Gate Fulford, when the army of Earls Edwin and Morcar attempted to defend the North against invasion by Harald Hardrada.
   a   Write down what Morcar's aims were, as Earl of Northumbria.
   b   Write down what Morcar's actions were.
   c   Write down what the outcome was.
   d   In what ways do the outcomes not live up to Morcar's expectations?
   e   Now imagine that you are Earl Morcar. Write a defence of your actions. Try to think about the things that you would have known about at the time and make sure that you do not use the benefit of hindsight.

3 'Arguments.' Work in groups of between four and six.
In turn, each group member will read out their defence. Other group members suggest ways to reassure the reader that they were not a failure and that, in some ways, what happened was a good outcome.

4 Think about King Harold and Harald Hardrada's invasion attempt.
   a   Write down what you think King Harold's aims were in September 1066. What actions did he take? What were the consequences?
   b   In what ways were the consequences of Hardrada's invasion not anticipated by King Harold?
   c   In what ways did Hardrada's invasion turn out better for King Harold (in the short-term) than he might have expected?

5 Think about Earl Tostig and Hardrada's invasion attempt of September 1066.
   a   In what ways were the consequences of the invasion attempt not anticipated by Tostig?
   b   In what ways did Hardrada's invasion attempt turn out worse for Tostig than their intended consequences?

6 To what extent are historical individuals in control of the history they helped to create? Explain your answer with reference to specific historical examples from this topic and others you have studied.

Exam-style question, Section B
Explain why there was a succession crisis after the death of Edward the Confessor.
You may use the following in your answer:
• Normandy   • the Witan
You **must** also use information of your own.   **12 marks**

Exam tip
This question is about causation. Six marks are for knowledge and understanding, six are for your analysis skills, so do not just describe what happened after January 1066. You need to identify the features of the succession crisis, then develop evidence to support each point.

38

Recap: Anglo-Saxon England and the Norman Conquest, 1060–66

Recall quiz

1   Who was the king of England before Harold?
2   Where was Harald Hardrada king of?
3   Name three of Harold Godwinson's brothers.
4   What was a burh?
5   What was the name for a 'free farmer' in Anglo-Saxon England?
6   List the four main claimants to the English throne after Edward died in January 1066.
7   Who won at Gate Fulford?
8   Who won at Stamford Bridge?
9   Name a tactic used by William at the Battle of Hastings.
10 Two of Harold's brothers died with him at the Battle of Hastings. What were their names and where were they earls of?

Source A

An Anglo-Saxon poem about a great English battle against the Vikings, which ended in an English defeat (the Battle of Maldon, 991), has a thegn saying:

I give you my word that I will not retreat
One inch; I shall forge on
And avenge my lord in battle.
Now that he has fallen in the fight
No loyal warrior living [...]
Need reproach me for returning home lordless
In unworthy retreat, for the weapon shall take me,
The iron sword.

Exam-style question, Section B
'The main reason for the English defeat at the Battle of Hastings was superior Norman tactics.'
How far do you agree? Explain your answer.
You may use the following in your answer:
• the feigned retreat
• the shield wall
You **must** also use information of your own.   **16 marks**

Exam tip
This is a question about cause. Remember that 'How far do you agree?' always means the need for analysis of points that support the statement and points that support other causes. The information provided to help you should be used in your answer, but remember that not using information of your own limits the number of marks.

Activity

1   Anglo-Saxons wrote epic poetry about bravery in battle and the honour of dying for their lord. Write a poem of your own, expressing the feelings of an Anglo-Saxon thegn who fought with Harold at the Battle of Hastings. Make it as epic as possible.
2   Put together a news-style report on the contenders for the throne of England following Edward's death in January 1066. Role-play interviews with the main contenders (make sure you use appropriate accents – you'll need a Hungarian accent for Edgar).
3   Draw a big concept map (spider diagram) for the topic: Reasons for William's victory. You will need to decide on some categories for your diagram – for example, tactics, luck, leadership, troops. Use A3 paper and colour-code your categories to help make them more memorable.

39

Our Student Books include '***Thinking Historically***' **activities** that target four key strands of understanding: evidence, interpretations, causation & consequence and change & continuity.

These are all based on the '*Thinking Historically*' approach we've developed in conjunction with Dr Arthur Chapman at the Institute of Education, University College London.

5

Timeline: Warfare

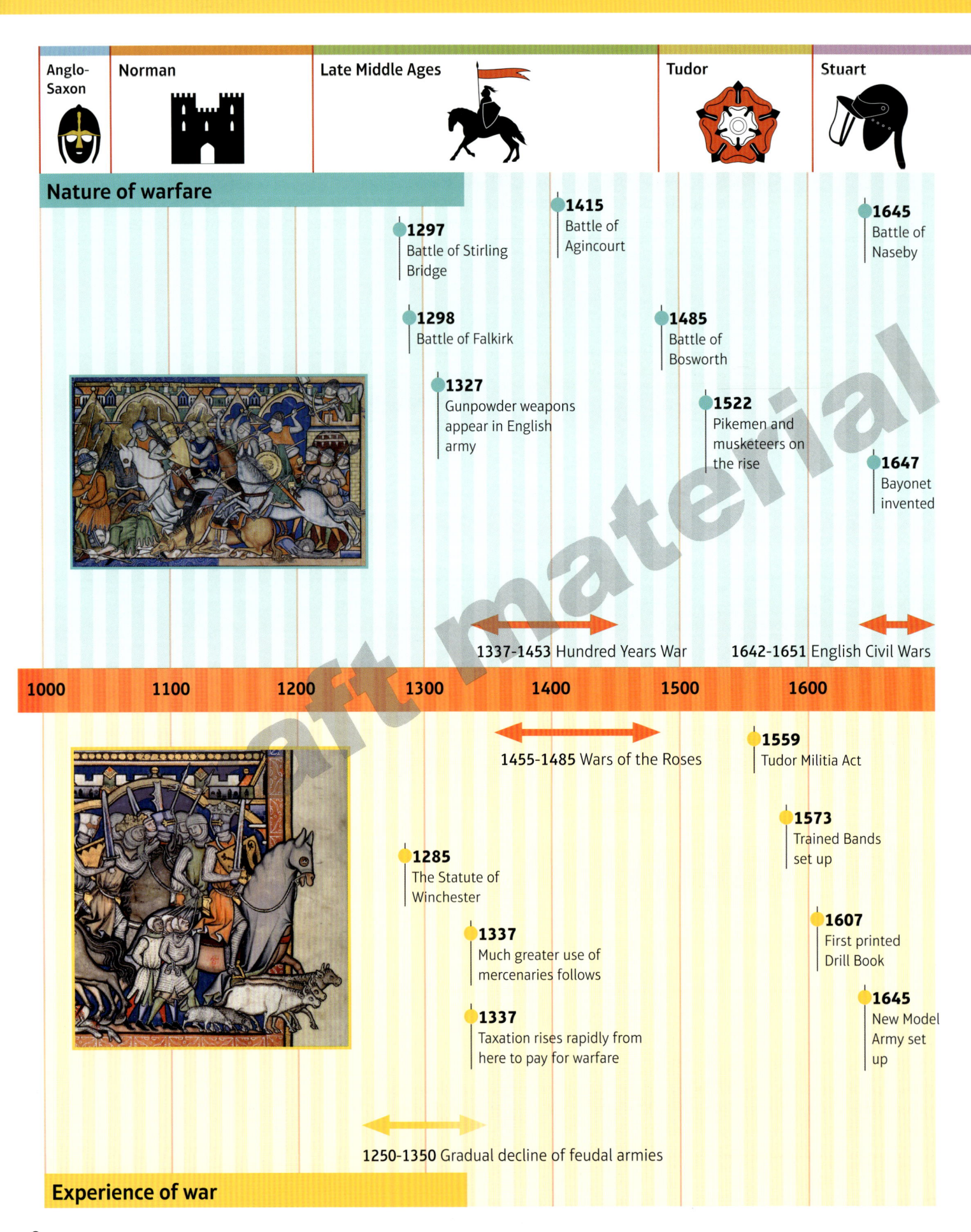

| Anglo-Saxon | Norman | Late Middle Ages | Tudor | Stuart |

Nature of warfare

- **1297** Battle of Stirling Bridge
- **1298** Battle of Falkirk
- **1327** Gunpowder weapons appear in English army
- **1415** Battle of Agincourt
- **1485** Battle of Bosworth
- **1522** Pikemen and musketeers on the rise
- **1645** Battle of Naseby
- **1647** Bayonet invented

1337–1453 Hundred Years War

1642–1651 English Civil Wars

1000 — 1100 — 1200 — 1300 — 1400 — 1500 — 1600

1455–1485 Wars of the Roses

- **1285** The Statute of Winchester
- **1337** Much greater use of mercenaries follows
- **1337** Taxation rises rapidly from here to pay for warfare
- **1559** Tudor Militia Act
- **1573** Trained Bands set up
- **1607** First printed Drill Book
- **1645** New Model Army set up

1250–1350 Gradual decline of feudal armies

Experience of war

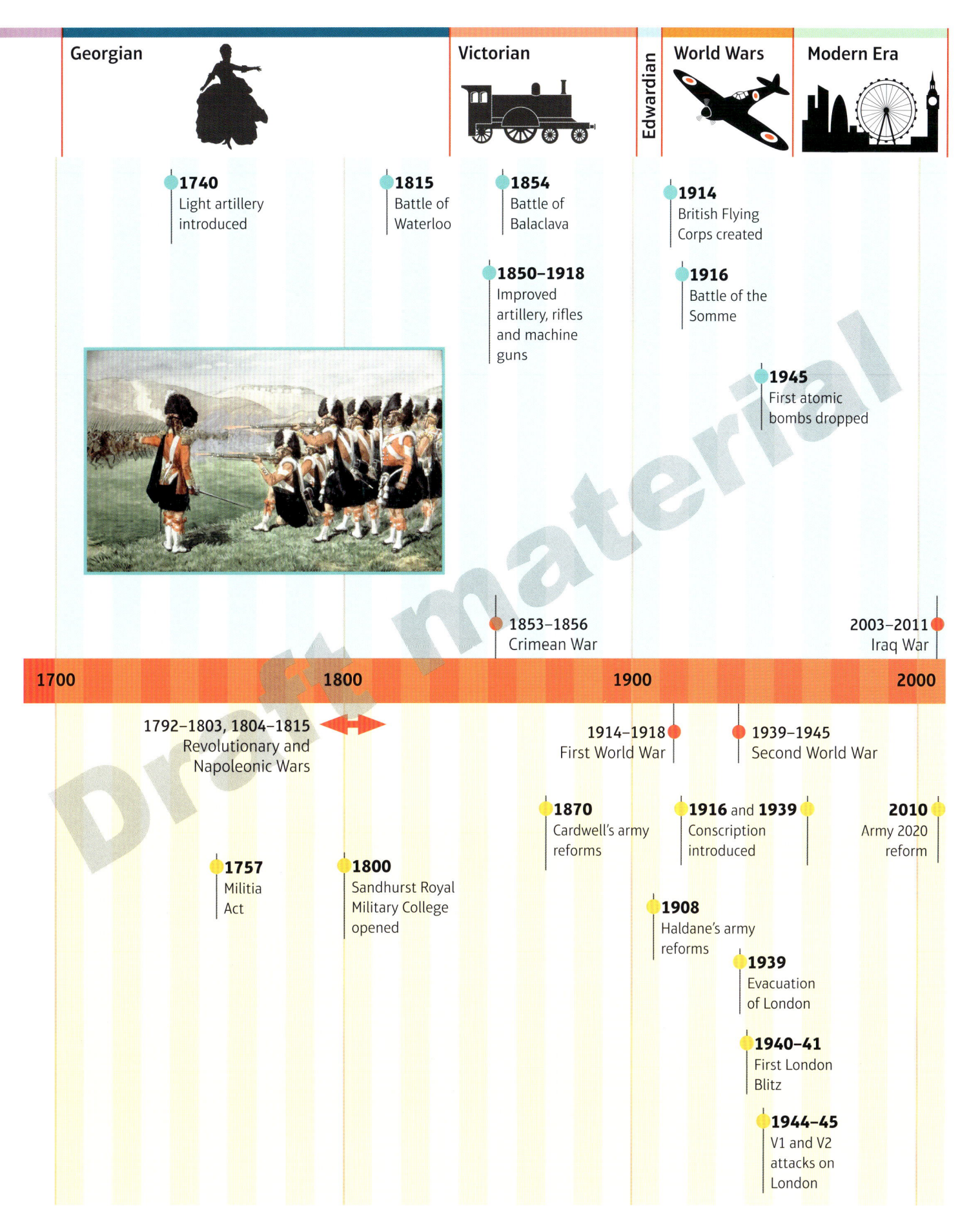

| Georgian | | Victorian | Edwardian | World Wars | Modern Era |

- **1740** Light artillery introduced
- **1815** Battle of Waterloo
- **1854** Battle of Balaclava
- **1850–1918** Improved artillery, rifles and machine guns
- **1914** British Flying Corps created
- **1916** Battle of the Somme
- **1945** First atomic bombs dropped

- **1853–1856** Crimean War
- **2003–2011** Iraq War

1700 — 1800 — 1900 — 2000

- **1792–1803, 1804–1815** Revolutionary and Napoleonic Wars
- **1914–1918** First World War
- **1939–1945** Second World War

- **1757** Militia Act
- **1800** Sandhurst Royal Military College opened
- **1870** Cardwell's army reforms
- **1916** and **1939** Conscription introduced
- **2010** Army 2020 reform
- **1908** Haldane's army reforms
- **1939** Evacuation of London
- **1940–41** First London Blitz
- **1944–45** V1 and V2 attacks on London

7

01 | c1250–c1500: Medieval warfare and English society

Between 1250 and 1500, England was almost constantly at war.
- Throughout this time, English kings fought for control of **Wales** and **Scotland**.
- From 1337–1453, England fought for land in France in the **Hundred Years' War**.
- From 1455–85, rival families fought for the throne in the **Wars of the Roses**.

During this time, many aspects of warfare remained much the same. Many of the same weapons, for example, were used in 1500 as much as they had been in 1250. Ultimately, battles continued to be won by hand-to-hand fighting amongst foot-soldiers.

However, some aspects of warfare changed. The rise of new weapons, like the longbow and cannon, changed the character of fighting on the battlefield, whilst the need for troops to serve in France brought an urgent need to change recruitment methods.

Sometimes change was gradual; sometimes it was sudden. There were several factors causing these changes. For example:
- Improvements in science and technology enabled the introduction of cannon.
- Changes in society, like the decline of feudalism, changed recruitment methods.

By comparing key events in the history of warfare during this time, through case studies like the Battles of Falkirk (1298) and Agincourt (1415), many of these changes can be seen in action.

Learning outcomes

By the end of this chapter, you will:
- know and understand what happened to the composition of armies, including the roles of infantry, archers and mounted knights, in this period
- understand the links between social structure and the command of armies
- know and understand the impact on warfare of new weapons, like the longbow and gunpowder weapons, and new tactics, such as those used by Scottish schiltrons
- understand the decline of the mounted knight
- know and understand what happened to recruitment, the training of combatants and the provisioning of armies, including requisitioning
- know and understand the impact of warfare on civilians.

Introduction: Warfare in c1250

Learning outcomes

- Understand the nature and experience of warfare in c1250.
- Understand how feudal society affected warfare.

The nature of warfare in c1250

Henry III was king of England in 1250. Henry fought a civil war against the English barons, and wars for control of Wales and parts of France. Henry's wars show us what warfare was like at that time.

The size of armies

In about 1250 in Britain, armies normally ranged from 5,000 to 10,000 men.

- When the barons rebelled against Henry III in 1264, their army contained 5,000 men.
- Henry's royal army totalled 8,000; his son, Edward, supported him with 2,000 more troops.

The composition of armies

Armies at this time usually had two parts, **infantry** and **cavalry**. The ratio varied, but the most common was 2:1, i.e. twice as many infantry as cavalry.

The cavalry were mounted soldiers. They were the elite of the army.

- Some cavalry were men from the upper nobility, like earls and dukes. The upper nobility formed about 30% of the cavalry at this time. Other cavalry were from the lesser nobility, like knights such as Sir Roger Bassett, who fought at the Battle of Falkirk in 1298.

- The rest of the cavalry were men-at-arms, heavily armed mounted troops brought to battle by the nobles. A nobleman's group – or **retinue** – of men-at-arms might vary from five to 25 men. They were usually men from the **gentry** – wealthy families who held land, but did not have titles.

The infantry were **common men** who fought as foot-soldiers. They were the bottom rung of the social ladder and were treated like second-rate troops in comparison with the mounted cavalry.

Social structure and the command of armies

The command of armies was directly linked to social structure.

- Kings rewarded supporters by granting them land. They became powerful nobles, leaders of society. In turn, they granted land to their supporters, lesser landowners, known as the gentry.
- In return, the nobles and the gentry were expected to command troops in support of the king.

So, command was decided more by **social position** than ability or experience, and the quality of command varied. Nobles were not used to being controlled, so cavalry sometimes ignored orders. For example, in 1264, at the Battle of Lewes, Prince Edward lost control of his cavalry. They abandoned King Henry's main attack and raided the enemy supply wagons instead. Meanwhile, the main attack failed.

Weapons and protection

In around 1250, cavalrymen and infantry fought with a variety of weapons:

- Cavalrymen normally took two horses each to war and fought on horseback. They would be armed with **lances** or thrusting **spears**, perhaps ten foot long, and **swords**.
- Most infantry had **swords** and **daggers**. Some had club-like weapons, like a **mace** or a **battle-axe**. Some used **halberds**, which were poles with axe-heads.

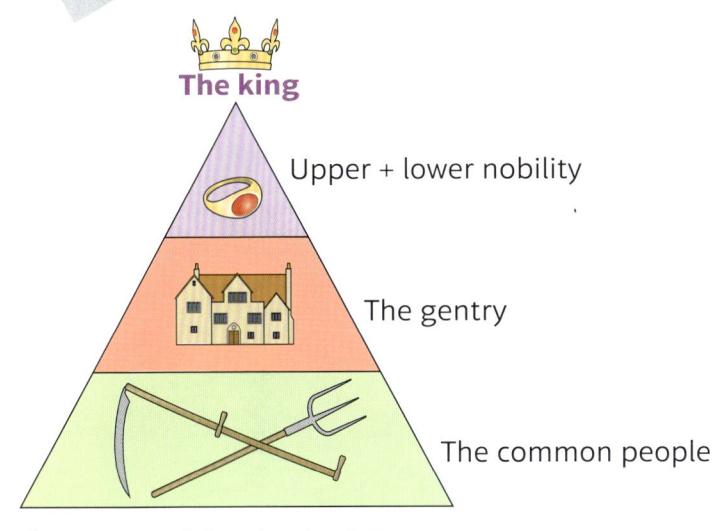

Figure 1.1 English society in 1250.

(Pyramid diagram: The king / Upper + lower nobility / The gentry / The common people)

Introduction: Warfare in c1250

- Some used '**brown bills**' – poles with broad-blades and a hook for hauling knights off their horses. Some carried pikes, long thrusting spears.
- Some infantrymen used **bows** or **crossbows**. Bows were about one metre long and could fire arrows about 100 metres. Crossbows were more powerful and very accurate, but slower to fire.

For protection, in around 1250:

- Most cavalrymen wore chainmail garments called **hauberks**. These had a hood – or **coif** – for the head and stretched as far as the knees. The knights, and sometimes horses too, often had colourful cloth **surcoats**. Flat-topped metal **helmets** were also worn and, by 1250, many of these had face-guards, with slits for ventilation and vision.
- Most infantrymen wore leather or padded linen jackets called **gambesons**. The best-defended infantry wore short mail shirts. Most infantry wore metal or leather **skull-caps**.

Activity

Study Source A and Source B (page 13). List the weapons and protective equipment you can see.

Strategy*

England in around 1250 was not democratic: the people had no say in government. It was controlled by kings and barons – and they needed to use **military force** to impose their decisions. Warfare, therefore, was a normal part of medieval society.

Kings and barons used warfare to stay in power; and they used force to seize power over others. There were two key features of military strategy they used to do this: **limited warfare** and the **use of castles**.

Key term

Strategy*

The overall plan used to achieve your objectives.

Limited warfare

Limited warfare was forced upon leaders by the nature of society at the time. For example:

- **Henry III had limited resources.** He could only raise quite small armies, with limited weapons.
- **He had limited power.** To raise an army, he had to persuade powerful nobles to support him.

Source A

An illustration from a Bible produced in about 1250. Although it is supposed to show a scene from the Bible, the artist used troops, weapons and a style of combat from his own time, so it is a useful source for historians of the period.

Introduction: Warfare in c1250

- **Battles were avoided** if possible. Since kings led armies, losing a battle might mean that a king was killed or captured and held for ransom (held prisoner until money was paid for his return).

Society in 1250 did not suit all-out warfare. Other aspects of society limited warfare too.

- **The campaigning season** – the months of the year when it was possible to fight – was limited. Most fighting took place from late spring, after people had sown crops, until autumn, when crops needed to be harvested and the weather made it much more difficult to move troops and to fight.
- **Communications** were limited. It was difficult for rival armies to know exactly where their opponents were. They had to rely on limited information from spies amongst the enemy or scouts using messengers, bugles, smoke signals, church bells and pigeons.

So, strategy in 1250 consisted of limited warfare. Commanders often preferred to **manoeuvre** the enemy into a hopeless position and then negotiate a victory; or besiege a **castle**; or attack enemy territory and destroy or steal **property** and **food**. Battles were a last resort.

For example, in the 1250s, Llewellyn the Last rejected Henry III's control of Wales. He avoided large battles by sending his forces, mobile bands of warriors, to ambush English troops, raid their camps and food supplies, and then slip away into the woods and mountains. This deliberately limited style of fighting is called **guerrilla warfare**.

Castles

Castles and fortified towns were an essential part of defensive strategy in 1250. If an army attacked an area defended by castles:

- The attackers had to **divide** their forces to besiege each castle.
- The defenders would have a series of **bases** from which to launch counter-attacks.

This put the attackers at a disadvantage. For example, in 1266, after the Battle of Evesham (1265), Henry III's enemies took refuge inside Kenilworth Castle, in Warwickshire; it took Henry's attacking army six months to get them out.

Source B

A 14th-century French manuscript showing how a strongly garrisoned castle could hold up an attacking army. The mail and style of helmets worn by the knights and small bows are typical also of the 13th century.

Introduction: Warfare in c1250

Extend your knowledge

Securing castles

In 1264, when Simon de Montfort rebelled against Henry III, Henry's first move was to secure the main Midland fortresses in the heart of the country; he then seized the castles at Tonbridge and Kingston, near the capital, London. Henry was taking care to secure key castles before confronting his enemy. Why did he do this?

Source C

Remains of the 11th century Kenilworth castle.

Tactics

Tactics are the way commanders use forces to get the upper hand.

Tactical formations

Setting up an army was an important part of tactics. For example, a commander could position his army on high ground, so that his enemy had to attack uphill. It was also important to protect the flanks (sides) of your infantry, so that enemy cavalry could not attack them from the side. Commanders could protect their flanks by positioning their own cavalry there or by setting up infantry where their flanks were protected by geographical features, such as woods or rivers.

At the Battle of Lewes (1264), Simon de Montfort placed his army on the crest of Offham Hill. His flanks reached sharp banks on the right and left, too steep for cavalry. The land in front was a long slope that the royal army had to climb.

Cavalry tactics

Cavalry were seen as the shock troops and dominant force on the battlefield. Their main tactics were:

- **The mounted charge.** At the Battle of Evesham (1265), Prince Edward used cavalry to target the enemy commander, Simon de Montfort. Mounted knights smashed through the enemy lines, engaged de Montfort's bodyguard and hacked him to pieces. It was a decisive move.

- **Rout and chase.** Cavalry tried to scatter enemy infantry. Once foot-soldiers ran, they were easy for mounted troops to chase and cut down. Often, more troops died fleeing than in the battle itself.

Infantry tactics

The infantry's task was to withstand any enemy attack and then overcome the enemy infantry.

- **The shield wall.** Men stood, with overlapping shields and spears or pikes, facing enemy attacks.

- **Archers.** Archers were used to weaken enemy troops. They usually played a minor role in tactics at this time. They had no significance in Henry III's battles at Lewes (1264) and Evesham (1265).

- **The mêlée.** If the archers and cavalry could not break the enemy, then the infantry would attack. Once infantry met, combat was frenzied hand-to-hand fighting, sometimes called a mêlée. Men slashed with swords, stabbed with spears and daggers, and crushed skulls and limbs with clubs.

Activities

1. Make a quiz about warfare in c1250 to test your classmates. The sections of the quiz should be 'The size and composition of armies', 'Cavalry', 'Infantry', 'Weapons and protection'. You must write out the questions and answers in full.

2. List four reasons why warfare in c1250 was on a limited scale. Decide the key reason and write a brief speech to explain why it was most important.

3. Have a 'speech-off' in a small group and decide the best reason from your list for Q2. At the end, record the winner and explain the reasons why.

4. Add a section to the quiz, which you began in the previous activity, to test your friends on tactics.

Introduction: Warfare in c1250

The experience of warfare in c1250

The **nature** of warfare tells us how armies were **made up**, **who** fought in them and **how** they fought. But what was the human **experience** of warfare in c1250?

Recruitment of cavalry

In about 1250, there were several ways that people could be recruited into Henry III's cavalry. The most common way depended upon the **feudal system**. This is an example of the way the nature of society affected warfare. It was a social system designed to provide and support troops.

Under the feudal system:

- The king granted his most powerful supporters control of large areas of England. They were usually earls or dukes, and were known as the king's **tenants-in chief**. They recognised the king as their lord and promised to give him military support.
- These tenants-in-chief granted control of some of their land to lesser nobles, known as **sub-tenants**. In return, they promised military support to the tenants-in-chief.

By 1250, the military support promised was measured as a number of knights, usually in fives or tens. This number was the **knight's fee**. A tenant may have promised a fee of one, five, 20 or 100 knights to his lord. **Knight service** was limited to 40 days' military service per year.

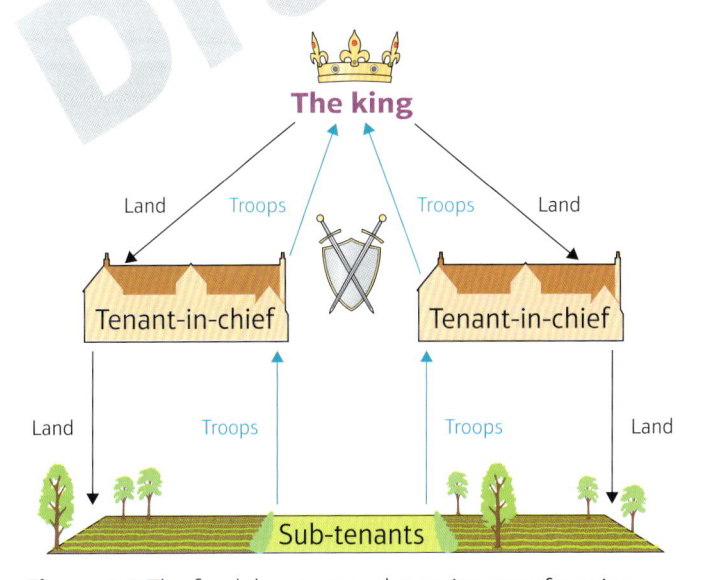

Figure 1.2 The feudal system and recruitment of armies.

Therefore, the way English society was **organised** had a major effect on the way armies were recruited.

Feudal knights

In 1250, most of Henry III's troops would have been feudal knights, serving their feudal duty to their lord. Henry III would have been able to call upon about 5,000 knights' fees, though they were rarely all called upon at once. Feudal troops made up the majority of the king's armies. However, by 1250, society was changing. The feudal system was breaking down. Kings found it hard to enforce their feudal dues. As a result, extra forms of recruitment were becoming more common.

The Assize of Arms

An extra way that kings used to recruit troops was the Assize of Arms. This assessed people's wealth to see if they should support the king with arms. It was a bit like taxation; the wealthier people were, the more military support they should give. For example, in 1250, Henry III was using an Assize of Arms that said that all men with land worth £15 had to supply him with a mounted knight, with a horse, hauberk, iron helmet, sword and dagger. Land worth £15 in 1250 would only be worth about £8,000 today, so many landowners in 1250 would have been required to fight in the king's army under this system.

Mercenaries and scutage

By 1250, kings found it difficult to force people to honour their feudal duties or accept the Assize of Arms. Because of this, kings routinely accepted money from people instead of military service. This payment was called **scutage**, or 'shield money'. This money was used by kings to pay for cavalry to fight alongside feudal troops. As a result, in 1250, Henry III was using scutage to employ paid troops, called **mercenaries**. These were employed, on a temporary basis, from **captains**, who were experienced soldiers that supplied units of 10 or 100 men for cash. Captains would charge about two shillings per day for mounted knights or one shilling for men-at-arms. Some of these were foreign troops, from Germany or France. Mercenaries were better trained, better disciplined and better armed than feudal troops, but much more expensive.

Introduction: Warfare in c1250

The Royal Household
A small number of troops were employed on a **permanent** basis. The Royal Household were permanent, paid troops who were employed to serve the king. It is estimated that Henry III had about 500 troops in his Royal Household. They were paid about £5 per year and one shilling per week extra on campaign. They were usually mounted troops.

Pay in 1250	Spending power of 1250 pay today
1 shilling	£25
2 shillings	£50
5 shillings	£125
20 shillings = £1	£500
£5	£2500

Recruitment of infantry
Feudal infantry
There had never been any feudal duty, like knight service, for ordinary people to serve the king in war as infantry. So, to recruit infantry, Henry III relied on a number of informal measures. For example:

- Some joined his army out of loyalty to their king or a desire to defend their country or region.
- Others joined for adventure or to escape poverty at home in exchange for regular food and even the chance of **plunder**: sometimes, when an enemy army or settlement was defeated, money and valuable goods could be stolen from bodies or houses and divided amongst the victorious army.

None of these methods produced big or well-equipped armies. A better source of men was the Assize of Arms.

The Assize of Arms
The Assize of Arms provided the beginnings of a reliable source of infantry. As well as demanding that wealthy men should serve the king as knights, it began to demand that all men of England should be ready to serve the king for 40 days, equipped with weapons, as troops in the infantry. For example, Henry III used the Assize of Arms to recruit infantry during the Barons' War of 1264–67. Commissioners of Array* visited selected parts of the country to assess people and to inspect their weapons. Often, local people shared the cost of equipping a few local volunteers, providing them with arms and enough supplies for 40 days' service.

Training
During the reign of Henry III, there were no permanent armies and no barracks (bases) for soldiers. As a result, there was little training for warfare.

For infantry, each issue of the Assize of Arms normally made it clear that those who answered the call to arms should be skilled at using their weapons. But, in practice, there was almost no organised training for infantry.

For cavalry, consisting of the nobility and the gentry, it was different. Amongst these classes, most young men were trained in military skills, especially horsemanship and the use of lances and other weapons. Young men competed to outshine each other at tournaments. A culture of chivalry* arose that dictated how knights should behave towards each other in combat. But, much of this was about individual combat. There was practically no training in how to fight in large, disciplined groups.

Key terms

Commissioners of Array*
Officials appointed by the king to organise the recruitment of troops under the Assize of Arms.

Chivalry*
A code of conduct adopted by medieval knights. In general social life, it involved politeness and courtesy, especially towards women. In war, it stressed bravery, loyalty and respect for the enemy.

Activities

1. In pairs, try to speak for a minute about the feudal system. Avoid hesitation, repetition or deviation.
2. Create a table about recruitment. The headings are 'Methods of Recruitment', 'Advantages', 'Disadvantages'. Create rows for 'Cavalry Recruitment' and 'Infantry Recruitment'. Discuss your table with others and then improve it.
3. List four ways in which what **English society** was like affected what **armies** and **warfare** were like in about 1250.

Introduction: Warfare in c1250

Provisioning

It was hard to provide food for armies and all their horses. There were a variety of solutions used.

- Men were expected to bring their **own provisions** for the first 40 days.
- **Baggage trains** of wagons, full of provisions paid for by the king, followed the armies.
- Sometimes, supplies were sent ahead by road or sea and stored in bases, known as **supply depots**, until the army arrived.
- Often, though, armies resorted to **demanding** supplies from local people. In home territory, they usually paid. In enemy territory, they often just stole what they needed.

Source D

An illustration from the Morgan Picture Bible, produced in about 1250. It shows an army taking prisoners, sheep and cattle by force. Like Source A, this illustration is of a scene from the Bible, but the artist used troops and weapons from his own time.

Summary

Warfare in c1250

- Armies around 1250 were **small** and consisted of **cavalry** and **infantry**.
- The **command** of armies was shaped by the class structure of English **society**.
- The two key aspects of strategy in warfare at this time were **limited warfare** and **castles**.
- Cavalry were recruited by **feudal duties**, the **Assize of Arms** and **paying** for troops.
- Infantry were recruited by appeals to **loyalty** and the **Assize of Arms**.
- **Training** was very limited for infantry; training for cavalry was more common for nobles.

Checkpoint

Strengthen

S1 Can you give examples of the size of armies in about 1250?

S2 Can you describe, in detail, the tactics of cavalry and infantry?

S3 What was the Assize of Arms and what kind of troops were paid in armies in about 1250?

If you are not confident about any of these questions, look up the answers on pages 11–16 and record them.

Challenge

C1 'Cavalry was the dominant force of the army in about 1250.' What are the arguments for and against this statement?

C2 How were the key features of English society in c1250 **linked** to the key features of: the command of armies, the strategy of armies, and the recruitment and training of armies?

If you are not confident about any of these questions, form a group with other students, discuss the answers and then record your conclusions. Your teacher can give you some hints.

15

1.1 The nature of warfare

> **Learning outcomes**
> - Understand the role of the infantry, archer and mounted knight in medieval armies.
> - Understand the impact on warfare of schiltrons, the longbow, gunpowder.
> - Understand the reasons for and impact of the decline of the mounted knight.

Change and continuity, 1250–1500

War was a **normal** part of medieval society, especially between 1250 and 1500.

- From 1250 to 1500, almost continuously, English kings fought for control of **Wales** and **Scotland**.
- From 1337 to 1453, England fought for land in France in the **Hundred Years' War**.
- From 1455 to 1485, rival families fought for the English throne in the **Wars of the Roses**.

Several aspects of warfare – though not all of them – changed during this intense fighting.

Continuity

The size of armies

The size of armies 1250–1500 is an example of **continuity** rather than change.

- In 1264, at the Battle of Lewes, the size of Henry III's army was about 10,000.
- In 1415, at the Battle of Agincourt, the size of Henry V's army was about 8,000.
- In 1485, at the Battle of Bosworth, the size of Richard III's army was about 12,000.

Strategy and command

Military strategy was another example of **continuity** in warfare during this time. Even though many battles were fought between 1250 and 1500, the two key features of English strategy stayed the same:

- Limited warfare. For example, during the Hundred Years' War, English armies carried out dozens of *chevauchees* – short raids on horseback by small armies of 2–3,000, intended to terrorise the local population and make it impossible for the French to raise taxes or grow crops.

> **Source A**
>
> English and Scottish infantry fighting at Bannockburn in 1314, from the Holkham Bible (c1320–30). The weapons and the hand-to-hand fighting that usually decided battles had not changed much since 1250.

- Capturing or building castles and fortified towns. For example, in the 1200s Edward I built castles in Wales to help him control his land there. In the 1400s, Henry V captured French castles at Harfleur and other French towns as bases from which he could control Normandy.

Another example of continuity was the command of armies. Throughout the period 1250 to 1500, kings continued to use their closest relatives and leading nobles as commanders of their armies.

- Edward I used the Earl of Surrey as his senior commander at the Battle of Falkirk in 1298.
- Henry V used the Duke of York as his senior commander at Agincourt in 1415.

Change

Schiltrons, and their impact on warfare

Pikes were wooden poles, three to five metres long, with metal tips, used by infantry to thrust at the enemy. Pikes were not new. They had mainly been used to defend infantry against attacks by cavalry. However, in this period, new uses for pikes emerged along with a new formation.

Scottish pikemen formed huge circles or squares of up to 2,000 men. These formations were called schiltrons. With pikes directed at the enemy, they were like huge, lethal hedgehogs.

- Schiltrons were a **natural** defensive formation: under attack, men tend to cluster together and horses were reluctant to charge a solid wall of pikes if the schiltron remained tightly packed.
- Getting men to **defend** with pikes was **normal**; however, getting pikemen to **advance**, in a group, to attack, was **harder** – and **new**. This is what the Scots did to defeat the English at the Battle of Stirling Bridge in 1297.

The Scots used schiltrons to defeat the English again at the Battle of Bannockburn in 1314 (see Source B). This time, the Scottish schiltrons advanced and defeated a force of English **cavalry**. It was a tactic that increased the power of the infantry; it also reduced the strength of the mounted knights because it showed that they could be defeated by attacking pikemen.

Extend your knowledge

The Battle of Stirling Bridge (1297)

The English and Scottish armies, both about 6,000 strong, faced each other across the River Forth. William Wallace was the leader of the Scottish rebels to the north of the river. He drew up his infantry, bearing pikes, in rectangular schiltrons, 100 men wide and six men deep.

- He watched whilst 2,000 English, mainly infantry, crossed a narrow bridge over the river.
- Before the English could organise after the crossing, Wallace surprised them. He used his schiltrons, not for defence, but for **attack**.
- Trapped and outnumbered, against the river bank, all but 300 English troops were killed.

Source B

In about 1350, Sir Thomas Gray, an English knight, wrote a history of England called *Scalacronica*. It is based on memories of relatives who fought in key battles. His father fought at the Battle of Bannockburn.

The... Scots came in a line of schiltrons and attacked the English columns, which were jammed together and could not operate against them... because their horses were impaled on the spikes. The troops in the English rear fell back into the ravine of the Bannock Burn, each tumbling one over the other.

Figure 1.3 An artist's impression of the bristling wall of spears of a Scottish schiltron.

1.1 The nature of warfare

One change – the use of pikes, organised in schiltrons to attack the enemy – was leading to another change in warfare: the decline of mounted knights (see page 24). Soon, that decline was accelerated by another change – the longbow.

The longbow and its impact on warfare

Longbows were used in Wales from about 1200. But, from about 1290, longbows started to be used in English armies. This was a change. Longbows were about two metres long, taller than most of the archers who used them. They were made from thick lengths of yew or elm wood. The archer held the arrow close to his ear before firing. This took great strength; so, it took a long time to train a longbow archer. However, they had several advantages:

- **Rate of fire:** a trained longbow archer could shoot ten to 15 arrows per minute – much quicker than the two to three shots of crossbows.
- **Distance:** a longbow was effective up to 200 metres, twice the range of shorter bows.
- **Power:** longbows were more powerful than shorter bows and crossbows. Their arrows were three feet long and could pierce armour. Records state that a longbow arrow once pierced a knight's mail, his thigh **and** his saddle, then killed his horse, leaving the knight pinned to the horse.

The effective use of large numbers of longbows was a feature of English armies for well over a century.

- In 1298, at the Battle of Falkirk, they helped King Edward I defeat the Scots.
- In battles such as Poitiers (1356) and Agincourt (1415), longbows were key to English victories over the French during the Hundred Years' War.

Longbows had become the dominant force on the battlefield. So, compared to 1250, the use of the longbow in battles was an important **change**. It also led to other changes. For example, it changed tactics, accelerated the decline of the mounted knight and changed armour (see below). This means that the longbow can also be said to be a **cause** of change.

Extend your knowledge

Poitiers (1356)

The archers of the English army at the Battle of Poitiers fired at least ten arrows per minute. One historian has estimated that English longbows launched 60,000 arrows at the French cavalry in just one minute. As a result, 40% of all the knights in the French army were killed.

Activities

In groups, come to a decision about the following questions. Record your decisions.

- a What was a pike and how was it normally used before the Battle of Stirling Bridge?
- b What was a schiltron?
- c What tactic did the Scots use, at the Battle of Stirling Bridge, that was unusual?
- d What impact did this new Scottish tactic have?

Figure 1.4: Modern drawing of 15th-century longbow archers.

Tactics changed

The power of the longbow created a change in the tactics of English armies, so that they could get the most out of this new weapon.

- **On the march**, archers rode on horseback – though they still fought on foot. This meant that the whole army could move at the speed of cavalry.
- In **attack**, before mounted cavalry charged, archers were still used to soften up the enemy – but they now did this with much greater effect.
- But, in **defence**, there was a change. English knights and men-at-arms dismounted to strengthen the centre of the defensive line, fighting on foot alongside the infantry. This meant that archers could be placed on the flanks. As the enemy attacked, they were met by showers of arrows, weakening their charge. The attackers were funnelled towards the men-at-arms. When the mêlée formed, the archers continued to fire into the flanks of the enemy forces and then joined in the mêlée.

This was the classic formation of many English victories, such as at Dupplin Moor and Agincourt.

Extend your knowledge

Dupplin Moor (1332)

At the Battle of Dupplin Moor, the Scots attacked the English army head-on. The dismounted English men-at-arms in the centre held firm, whilst longbow archers advanced on the flanks and poured arrows into the Scots. Unable to retreat because of the bodies of the men killed by arrows, the Scots were trapped in a hail of arrows and almost wiped out. The Scots lost three earls, 58 knights, 1,200 men-at-arms and thousands of infantry.

The composition of armies changed

The success of the longbow changed the composition of the English army.

- Armies began to have more infantry and fewer cavalry. In about 1250, the normal ratio of infantry to cavalry was 2:1. By about 1400, it was 3:1.
- The dominance of cavalry was reduced. This had already been dented by Scottish schiltrons. Their value was now reduced by the importance of archers.

Armour changed

The use of the longbow also led to change in the protection troops wore.

Plate armour: From about 1300, chainmail was reinforced by adding plates of metal. First, breastplates covered the chest. Then plates were added to protect shoulders, elbows, hands, knees, shins and feet.

Suits of armour: By about 1420, the whole body was covered and whole suits of armour developed.

Armour protected the wearer from slashing swords. However, it only gave limited protection against arrows. Many of the French at the Battle of Poitiers (1356) wore plate armour and they still died in large numbers. And it was even less useful against firearms (see page 23).

Extend your knowledge

Roger's tomb

In 1298, a brass tomb engraving was made of Roger of Trumpington, showing him in chainmail.

In 1325, a similar engraving shows John of Creke wearing a type of helmet called a bassinet and plate armour, including a **cuirass**, **brassarts**, **poleyns**, **greaves**, **sabatons** and **gauntlets**.

Do an Internet search to find out what these items were. Look for them in Source A on page 27.

Activities

Think about the way longbows came to be used and what changes they caused.
1. Write a paragraph starting: 'The use of longbows was a **change** in warfare because…'
2. Write a paragraph starting: 'The use of longbows was a **cause of change** because…'
3. In a group, discuss this question: How does change happen? Jot down your conclusions.

1.1 The nature of warfare

Gunpowder and its impact on warfare

In 1250–1320, people knew about gunpowder, but it was hardly used by English armies.

Gunpowder was first made by the Chinese in about 900AD. By 1250, there were some people in Europe who were interested in science and experimented with chemicals so that they could copy the Chinese. An English friar, Roger Bacon, was one of these. In 1267, he wrote that gunpowder had a roar greater than thunder and a flash greater than lightning.

Cannon, 1320–1430

During this time, the technology of making cannon began, but they had little military significance.

- Some of the very earliest cannon had wooden barrels, reinforced with metal bands, and shot lumps of stone, sculpted into balls.
- **In 1327**, Edward III's army used cannon against the Scots. The first English illustration of a cannon appeared in the same year.
- **In 1346**, the English army used cannon during the Hundred Years' War against France. They were used in the siege of Calais and in the Battle of Crècy, but they made little impact. A contemporary writer said that the English merely 'fired off some cannons to frighten' the enemy.
- **In 1415**, Henry V used 12 cannon to besiege the castle at Harfleur. But, after five weeks, the walls remained intact. The town eventually gave up because its food supplies had been cut off.

Source C

The English army's siege of Berwick, in 1333, described in a chronicle (a contemporary history of the time). The author is unknown.

They made many assaults with guns and other [siege] engines... wherewith they destroyed many a fair house; and churches were also beaten to the earth with great stones that pitilessly came out of the guns... [but the enemy] abided there so long, till those that were in the town failed victuals [ran out of food].

From these examples, it's clear that cannon were not a dominant force in warfare. In the 1320s, they had an effective range of only 100 yards. They were also heavy

Source D

A manuscript illustration from a 15th-century chronicle, showing the use of cannon and mortars to attack the city of Bordeaux, during the Hundred Years' War between England and France.

and therefore slow to transport around battlefields. For this reason, they were mainly used in sieges during this period.

Cannon, 1430–1500

By 1430, cannon were improving. **Technology** was the reason.

- **Metal was used.** Foundries, which made metal goods, used skills honed in making church bells to experiment with iron, copper, bronze and brass barrels. Metal cannon balls gradually replaced stone.
- **Design improved.** At first, barrels were not much longer than their diameter. By 1430, as technology improved, they were sometimes three times as long as their diameter, giving greater accuracy, power and range.

- **Trunnions were invented.** These were rods at each side of the barrel that allowed the barrel to be lifted into higher or lower slots on the frame of the cannon. This made it easier to adjust the height and distance of fire.
- **Specialist cannon were made.** These included light, mobile cannon; heavy cannon, or **bombards**, to fire stone balls weighing half a ton; and **mortars** or **howitzers** to lob missiles high over castle walls.

The impact of improved cannon

Sometimes cannon were useful in battles. At the Battle of Castillon (1453), 1,000 English cavalry took heavy losses from French cannon. However, cannon were mainly useful in sieges. Tall castle and city walls were suddenly vulnerable. Henry V's 12 cannon had failed for five weeks to defeat Harfleur in 1415. But, because of improvements in cannon, in 1449 Harfleur fell to attack by 16 French cannon after only 17 days. So, castle walls needed to be thicker and shorter to withstand cannon and make them harder to knock down.

Firearms, 1400 onwards

During the 15th century, firearms were developed. These were gunpowder weapons that could be carried and fired by individuals. Firearms like the **arquebus** (sometimes called the **hackbut**) became common on the battlefield in Europe. In 1490, Venice replaced all crossbows with arquebuses.

However, it is difficult to argue that gunpowder weapons – whether cannon or firearms – were a key force in English warfare by 1500.

Cannon were:

- unreliable – in 1460, King James II of Scotland was killed when one of his own cannon blew apart
- slow to re-load and inaccurate over long distances
- only really useful in sieges; they were very heavy to manoeuvre for battles.

Firearms were:

- slow to load (powder and shot had to be rammed down the barrel, a smouldering piece of rope had to be kept alight to ignite the powder)
- unreliable (firing could fail in damp weather)
- used very little by English armies before 1500. (The longbow was so successful that firearms were adopted more slowly in England than in other parts of Europe.)

At the Battle of Bosworth (1485), where many cannonballs were recovered from the battlefield, there is almost no evidence of shot from firearms at all.

> ### Activities
>
> 1. Make a timeline of key periods and events in the use of gunpowder weapons, 1250–1500.
> 2. Draw a graph. Label the horizontal axis '1250 to 1500'. The vertical axis represents how important gunpowder weapons were: not important at the bottom, very important at the top. Draw a line to show how the importance of gunpowder weapons changed, 1250–1500.
> 3. How did the following affect the development of gunpowder weapons?
>   a science   b technology
> 4. Consider this statement: 'There was great progress in gunpowder weapons, 1250–1500.' List the reasons you agree and the reasons you disagree. What is your overall conclusion?

The decline of the mounted knight

In about 1250, the mounted knights of the cavalry were the cream of the English army. They were:

- a **large** part of the army
- its key **tactical** force
- its social and military **leaders**.

By 1500, their dominance in all these areas had not disappeared entirely, but had declined.

Reasons for change

In about 1250, the mounted charge was often the key to victory. Cavalry were the tanks of medieval times. If possible, they were the decisive shock force that punched through opposition defences. If this did not work, they weakened and disrupted the enemy before the infantry engaged.

But, from about 1290, the role of cavalry was changed by a **combination** of reasons.

- **Pikes** were used, not just to **defend** against cavalry but even to **attack** and defeat it.
- **Longbows** weakened the enemy infantry better than cavalry and could also destroy cavalry.

1.1 The nature of warfare

- **Cannon** and **firearms** later began to do the same jobs as longbows.

As a result, the cavalry's place in English armies changed.

Tactical change
Cavalry tactics changed. From about 1330, the English army learned to use cavalry differently. Instead of acting alone, as an elite strike force, cavalry were used as part of an **integrated** force, working alongside other types of troops. During the Hundred Years' War, they:

- took **specialist** tasks, like patrolling, foraging for food, scouting and raiding
- **dismounted** in battle, joining the infantry in defence, while archers weakened the enemy charge
- **mounted** and chased down fleeing troops, once the enemy's attack was repelled.

This was an important role. But not the **separate**, **superior** role cavalry had held before. The French did not make this change. This is an important reason for English victories, like Crècy, Poitiers and Agincourt, during the Hundred Years' War.

Numbers change
The number of cavalry in armies changed.

- By about 1400, the ratio of cavalry to infantry had changed from 1:2 in 1250, to about 1:3. For example, the 1370 campaign to France had 1,500 mounted cavalry and 4,000 archers.
- In Henry VI's campaigns in France in the 1440s, the ratio averaged 1:10.

Change in social structure
The social class and command of cavalry changed.

- In about 1250, with the feudal system the main means of recruitment, about 30% of English cavalry were from the **nobility**. But, as the feudal system declined, many knights paid scutage instead of fighting. Only 5% of cavalry were nobles for the English campaign in France in 1375.
- More mercenaries were employed as mounted men-at-arms. They had their own leaders (or captains). This weakened the link between social class and **command**.

Exam-style question, Section B

The use of pikes was the most important reason for the decline of mounted knights, 1250–1500.

How far do you agree? Explain your answer.

You may use the following in your answer:

- schiltrons
- the longbow

You **must** also use information of your own. **16 marks**

Exam tip

This question tests analysis and evaluation of causation and consequence. Your answer must be written as an argument, for and against the statement in the question, and you must give evidence and examples to back up your points. To get top marks you also need to include information of your own.

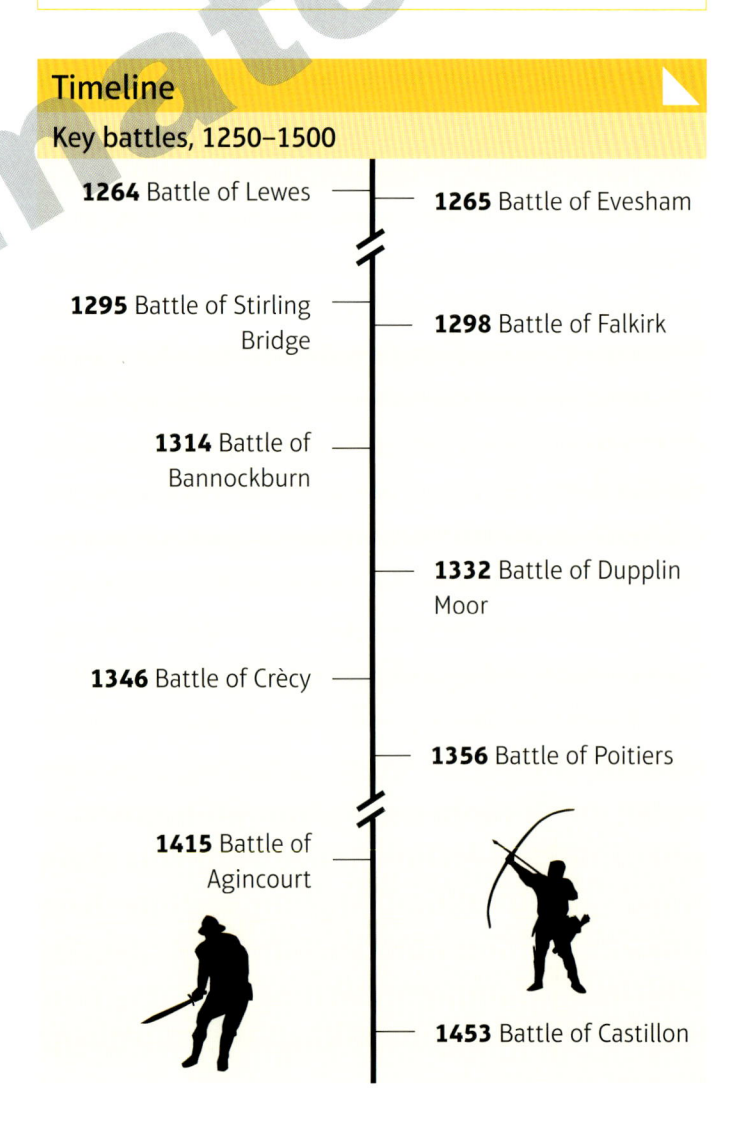

Timeline
Key battles, 1250–1500

- **1264** Battle of Lewes
- **1265** Battle of Evesham
- **1295** Battle of Stirling Bridge
- **1298** Battle of Falkirk
- **1314** Battle of Bannockburn
- **1332** Battle of Dupplin Moor
- **1346** Battle of Crècy
- **1356** Battle of Poitiers
- **1415** Battle of Agincourt
- **1453** Battle of Castillon

1.1 The nature of warfare

By 1500, the mounted knight still had a role in English armies and the mounted charge was still a fearsome force. A mounted knight (150lb), with his armour (up to 60lb) and weapons (40lb), bearing down on the enemy at 15 miles per hour was a frightening sight. When you add the weight of the horse, this totalled well over half a ton (500kg). Even against longbows and firearms, the mounted knight still struck with great power. However, the elite cavalry of around 1250 was a **smaller**, **socially different** and more **flexible** force by 1500.

Activities

Make a table with four columns. The four headings are 'Date', 'Battle', 'Combatants', 'Key Features'. Look back through this section for information about each battle.

1. In the 'Combatants' column, write details of the leaders and armies involved.
2. In the 'Key Features' column, list any details of the battle that you could use as examples of a special feature of warfare at this time, e.g. 'undisciplined cavalry lost Henry the battle'; 'pikes used to defeat cavalry'; 'longbows were the decisive weapon'.
3. Use the battles to give an example of something that changed in warfare, 1250–1500. Then use them to give an example of something that did not change, 1250–1500.

THINKING HISTORICALLY — Cause and Consequence

The language of causation

Study these words and phrases. They are useful in describing the role of causes and how they are related to each other and to events.

motivated	precondition	prevented	determined the timing	deepened the crisis	led to
exacerbated	allowed	triggered	impeded	catalyst	developed
underlying	created the potential	influenced	enabled	accelerated	sparked

1. Create a table with the following column headings: 'word', 'meaning', 'timing'. Write out each word or phrase in a separate row of the 'word' column.
2. Discuss the meaning of each word or phrase with a partner. For each word or phrase, write a short definition in the 'meaning' column.
3. Is each word or phrase more likely to describe a short-term, medium-term or long-term cause? In the 'timing' column, write "short", "medium" or "long".
4. Look at the following incomplete sentences. Write three versions of each sentence, using different words and phrases from the table above to complete them. You can add extra words to make the sentences work. For each sentence, decide which version is the best.
   a. The development of longbows and cannon….the decline of the mounted knight
   b. The decline of the feudal system…changes in recruitment to armies
   c. The long bow…the English victory at Agincourt.
5. You can also describe the importance of causes. Place the words below in order of importance. You should put words that suggest a cause is very important at the top, and words that suggest a cause is less important at the bottom of your list.

| necessary | contributed to | added to | marginal | fundamental | influenced |
| supported | negligible | | | | |

23

1.1 The nature of warfare

Source E

An illustration from Sir Thomas Holme's Book of Arms, dating from about 1480. It shows two knights in armour and colourful tabards (coat or tunic) practising their sword-play at a tournament.

Summary

The nature of warfare, 1250–1500

- England was involved in almost continuous warfare from 1250–1500.
- The size of armies, many weapons and military strategy are examples of continuity in warfare.
- The use of the pike, especially in schiltrons, as an attacking tactic is an example of change.
- The longbow and its impact on armour, and army composition and tactics, is also change.
- Gunpowder weapons and their impact on warfare is an example of change.
- The decline of the mounted knight is also an example of change.
- New weapons and changes in science and technology were factors that caused change.

Checkpoint

Strengthen

S1 Can you give examples of continuity in army size, weaponry and strategy during this period?

S2 Can you describe, in detail, how pikes and schiltrons were used for attack at this time?

S3 Can you describe, in detail, how longbows were used and what difference this made?

S4 Can you describe, in detail, the development of gunpowder weapons and their impact to 1500?

If you are not confident about any of these questions, look up the answers in page 18–24 and record the answers for future reference.

Challenge

C1 Can you explain how **a combination of factors** changed the role of mounted knights?

C2 Can you explain how changes in **science** and **technology** caused change during this period?

If you are not confident about any of these questions, form a group with other students, discuss the answers and then record your conclusions. Your teacher can give you some hints.

1.2 The experience of warfare

> **Learning outcomes**
> - Understand how medieval armies recruited and trained their soldiers.
> - Understand how medieval armies were supplied and provisioned.
> - Understand the impact of warfare on English civilians at this time.

Change and continuity, 1250–1500

Recruitment

In about 1250, when recruiting **cavalry**, kings used:

- the **feudal duty** of nobles and knights
- the **Assize of Arms** to demand military service from the wealthy
- **paid troops**, like the Royal Household and mercenaries.

In about 1250, when recruiting **infantry**, kings relied on:

- the **loyalty** or desire of common people to defend their homeland
- the **Assize of Arms** to demand military service from poorer men.

Recruitment, 1250–1500

What happened to recruitment 1250–1500 is that:

- **feudal troops** continued to be used until about 1350
- the **Assize of Arms** was used **more** after 1285, and then continually to 1500
- **payment** for troops was used **more** after 1337, and became the main way of recruiting.

Feudal troops

Kings and tenants-in-chief called upon their sub-tenants to provide knight service until about 1330. In 1322, Edward II invaded Scotland with 500 troops fulfilling feudal dues. The last summons of feudal troops was in 1327.

There were too many disadvantages to feudal troops.

- Until about 1330, kings could call upon 5,000 mounted feudal troops. But this was quite a small number and it limited the size of armies.
- Feudal troops were only required to fight in England and only for 40 days. For more, they expected pay.

> **Source A**
>
> Sketch of the tomb of Sir Edmund Thorpe. He was recruited to fight in the armies of a number of English kings. He died on campaign in France in 1418.
>
> - In 1385, he was part of the **feudal** retinue of Sir John Wingfield.
> - In 1392, he was a **Commissioner of Array** for Richard II.
> - In 1399, he was in the **Royal Household** of Henry IV.

25

1.2 The experience of warfare

- The quality of feudal troops was unreliable. They trained very little and the ability of their leaders varied, since they were chosen by social status rather than experience. Added to this, the discipline of feudal knights was unreliable.
- Feudal infantry were part-time soldiers and the quality of their weapons was poor.

Also, society was changing. The feudal system was breaking down. Tenants could no longer be relied upon to honour feudal duties. So, as society changed, recruitment had to change too.

Assize of Arms
As feudal loyalty declined, kings tried to compel men to join their armies by other means. In 1285, the system of raising troops by the Assize of Arms was clarified and extended by Edward I in **The Statute of Winchester**. This ordered:

- **Commissioners of Array** would be appointed for each town and county.
- These would annually **muster** (gather) all local able-bodied men aged 16–60; this gathering was called the array of arms.
- Every man, however poor, had to bring at least a bow, 24 arrows, a sword and a dagger.
- Wealthier men had to provide armour, a shield, lance, sword and dagger, and a warhorse.
- Men were then selected to serve for 40 days. For longer, or for campaigns abroad, they were paid. This meant that, apart from local defence, they effectively became **paid** troops.

Recruitment by Assize of Arms continued throughout this whole period. In 1457, for example, in the Wars of the Roses, 180 foot-soldiers mustered in Bridport, in Dorset. However, it is not clear how far people actually complied with the Assize of Arms. For example, in 1296, a list of 713 men were summoned to serve Edward I in France; only 76 actually sailed.

Paid troops
Because kings could never raise the quantity or quality of troops they needed by **compelling** people to fight, either by feudal dues or by the Assize of Arms, they increasingly relied on **paying** for troops.

The Royal Household
Because kings had to rely more heavily on paid troops, the size and importance of the Royal Household gradually increased between 1250 and 1500.

- In 1250, Henry III had a Royal Household of about 500 mounted cavalry.
- By 1300, his son, Edward I, had a Royal Household of about 4,000.

Mercenaries
The need for armies increased during the Hundred Years' War, after 1337. So, this was the period when paying for troops became the main method of recruiting. Edward III's army of 1337 was the first English army to consist **entirely** of paid troops.

Typically, the king's agents would enter into a contract – or **indenture** – with a captain who could provide a body of troops for a fee. These captains then paid the men. For example, in 1346, the year of the Battle of Crecy, Thomas Dagworth, a famous captain, supplied King Edward III with 300 men-at-arms and 600 archers. For this, he was paid 2,500 marks – the equivalent of over half a million pounds today.

Sometimes, the commanders and troops would be the very same men who would have served the king under the feudal system. So, the role of the nobility in the English army did not disappear.

Activities

Draw a graph. The bottom axis of your graph covers the years 1250–1500.

1. Use pages 27–28 to plot lines to show how important the following were during this period: (i) Feudal troops (ii) The Assize of Arms (iii) Paid troops.
2. Write a paragraph to explain each of the lines.
3. Historians sometimes use the word 'trend' when describing change. A trend is the **general direction** of change. So, for example, we could say about the world today that the trend is for computers to become more and more important in modern life. Write a paragraph to explain how paying troops rather than compelling troops was a trend in recruitment, 1250–1500.

1.2 The experience of warfare

From compulsion to payment
Compelling people to fight, by feudal dues or Assize of Arms, worked less and less well after 1250. **Paying** troops was not new in 1250, but it was the main recruiting method by 1500. This was a **change**.

> **Exam-style question, Section B**
> Explain **one** way in which recruitment was different by c1500 than it had been in c1250. **4 marks**

> **Exam tip**
> This question tests knowledge and understanding of difference, features and characteristics. In your answer, you only need to give one way in which recruitment was different by 1500 than it had been in 1250, but to get all of the marks you must give evidence or examples to support what you are saying.

Training
New recruitment methods after 1250 led to better training. But there is no record that any new books of military tactics were produced in England in the period 1250–1500. It seems that the command and organisation of troops remained very simple.

Feudal troops were only summoned for war. Knights practised combat at tournaments. But there was no training for groups of knights. There was no peacetime training for feudal infantry at all.

The Assize of Arms made troops slightly better prepared for war.

- At the annual array of arms, men mustered for inspection by the king's Commissioner of Array. This was a chance to check the quality of weapons and equipment and practise using those weapons.
- In 1285, Edward I's Statute of Winchester insisted that archery targets were set up in every town.
- In 1363, Edward III ordered that there should be archery practice on all feast days and holidays.

Paid troops were better trained. By the 1400s, they were the troops kings preferred for campaigning.

- They were experienced men, fighting in fixed groups and with the same commanders. Paid archers were trained by **centanaurs**, leaders of 100 men, to fire volleys (large groups) of arrows onto targets.
- Kings often insisted on regular musters to inspect paid troops – so that they could be sure that they were getting good value for money. These musters were used to organise training.

Provisioning and requisitioning
The need for armies to have food and equipment was not new. However, from 1250 to 1500, provisioning became more important. There was a **combination** of factors causing this.

- **More war.** England was almost constantly at war from 1250–1500.
- **More horses.** Cavalrymen in about 1250 each took two warhorses on campaign. By the 1300s, they took four and archers also rode horses. This added up to thousands of horses, all needing fodder.
- **More weapons.** At the Battle of Crècy, in 1346, English archers shot half a million arrows in a day. Once gunpowder weapons came in, troops could no longer supply their own ammunition.

> **Source B**
> An illustration in a prayer book called *Luttrell's Psalter*, from about 1340, showing archery practice.

1.2 The experience of warfare

So, kings had to use a variety of methods to make sure that their armies had enough supplies.

Requisitioning*

Food and fodder for the army was requisitioned by the Crown by compulsory purchase all around the country. This process was called **purveyance**. It was supposed to pay a fair price to the owners.

Supplies were then sent, usually by sea, to supply depots.

- In 1297, supplies were sent over 500 miles from the Isle of Wight to Scotland.
- Chester served as a supply depot for campaigns in Wales; Berwick for Scotland.

Food provisioning often didn't work. Armies would have to resort to foraging in the countryside and plundering (stealing) food from others, like farmers, local landowners or even monasteries. On many occasions, armies went short of food for weeks.

Source C

An English illustration c1500 showing the baggage train of the king of Sicily.

Key term

Requisitioning*

A requisition was a formal order from the authorities for private property or goods to be handed over to the military forces for their use. Usually, the goods requisitioned would be paid for – but not always.

The Royal Armoury

Weapon stores were also created. During the Hundred Years' War, the Crown began to order large quantities of weapons and store them in the Royal Armoury, based in the Tower of London.

Before 1307, under Edward I, archers supplied their own arrows. By 1360, the Royal Armoury stored 11,000 bows and half a million arrows. In the 1380s, the Crown also bought 87 cannon.

Baggage trains

On campaign, armies transported supplies in baggage trains, convoys of wagons and pack animals that followed the army. This baggage train would have to carry the army's weapons, armour, tent canvas, tent poles, tools, cooking equipment and food. An army of 15,000 men would need over 100 carts in its baggage train. The carts were pulled by horses, which also needed to be fed, making the problem of finding enough provisions even harder. Baggage trains also slowed the army down; they could only move at about 15 to 20 miles per day. If an army's baggage train was destroyed, it risked starving. This is why the enemy baggage train was often a target for attack.

The impact of warfare on civilians

Medieval warfare had an impact on civilians in a variety of ways. The impact was mainly bad. The three main impacts were caused by the **cost** of warfare, **recruitment** for wars and the impact of **fighting** during wars.

The cost of warfare

England was almost constantly at war between 1250 and 1500 – and wars were expensive. Kings had to build castles, pay troops, and pay for their weapons and supplies. The ways in which kings raised the money and supplies they needed had a bad impact on civilians in the following ways.

Increased taxation

Kings constantly raised taxes during this period (see the table below). The tax burden on the population almost doubled between 1337 and 1422. Paying extra taxes caused citizens hardship.

This is in part shown by the Peasants' Revolt in 1381, as one reason for the revolt was unrest about taxes. However, the burden of taxation should not be exaggerated; even at the end of the Hundred Years' War, tax was only about 1% of annual income for most people.

King	Tax collected per year	Modern value
Edward III (1337–77)	£75,000	£32 million
Richard II (1377–99)	£100,000	£45 million
Henry V (1413–22)	£125,000	£60 million

Purveyance

One way kings paid for the cost of wars was purveyance – requisitioning food and supplies. When the Crown requisitioned food, it was supposed to pay a fair price. It often didn't. It rarely paid in cash. It usually paid in wooden 'tallies' – a kind of IOU. Paying off the tallies took months or years. Giving away their goods and not getting paid for ages must have caused civilians great hardship. A popular poem of 1340 indicates that it was a cause of resentment. It said: 'You who eat off silver and pay in wood, how much better to pay in silver and eat off wood.'

Seizing ships

As well as food, kings also requisitioned goods, such as ships for transport. To send armies and supplies to campaign in France required many ships. In 1346, for the Crécy campaign, the Crown had no ships of its own, so 700 private ships were seized instead.

Recruitment

A second way in which warfare affected citizens was recruitment. People were compelled to fight. The feudal summons to fight for the king and the Assize of Arms were both ways of forcing people to join armies. It is clear that, during the period 1250 to 1500, civilians did not like being forced to fight:

- An increasing number chose to pay money – scutage – instead of going to war themselves.
- Some civilians who answered the call to arms deserted at the first opportunity. For example, in 1300, of 9,000 troops who mustered with the army in Scotland, only 5,000 remained after one month.
- Some civilians just refused to serve. In 1355, when archers from Gloucester were told to join the king's army in Scotland, they just refused.

The impact of fighting

Medieval strategy and tactics also meant that civilians suffered **during** wars. Sometimes, instead of fighting the enemy's army, attacking forces attacked civilians instead (see Interpretation 1).

Interpretation 1

Description of raids on enemy land from *The Cambridge History of Warfare*, edited by historian G. Parker (2005).

The principal aim was to weaken the enemy's morale and ability to pay taxes, and to break his resolve. [The] prime targets were population, economy and social infrastructure rather than armies.

Raids

Sometimes armies raided towns and villages in enemy territory. This caused suffering and panic amongst the civilian population. It also made the enemy's leaders and their army look weak. In 1296, a Scottish army raided the north of England. Contemporary sources say that they killed 'infirm people, old people and women in child-bed' and that, in Corbridge, '200 scholars were in a school; having blocked up the doors, (the Scots) set fire to the building'. Sometimes this tactic caused enough suffering amongst civilians that the invading army were paid or given land to go away.

Plunder and destruction of property

Armies often stole supplies from the land in enemy territory (see Source D). This had two benefits for the attackers. It gave them an extra source of food and it deprived their enemy of food. But it also deprived civilians of food, which could lead to starvation.

1.2 The experience of warfare

Source D

From a medieval French history book showing infantry looting a house in France in about 1375.

Ransoms

Sometimes, on campaign, an army might not attack a town. Instead, they would camp nearby and demand money from the town in exchange for a promise not to attack. Soldiers occasionally kidnapped civilians and held them to ransom (money demanded for the return of prisoners). For example, in 1380, 168 civilians were seized in a French town, Bergerac, and forced to pay for their freedom. Fear of being taken captive during warfare must have caused terror amongst civilians.

Sieges of towns and castles

Besieging castles and fortified towns was a key strategy in warfare at this time. This involved cutting off food and water supplies, and attacking with siege weapons or cannon. This caused great suffering to civilians inside. For example, when Henry V besieged the French town of Rouen in 1418–19, he chose to starve the town into surrender. Contemporary chroniclers claim that, by the time the town surrendered, townspeople were dying faster than carts could carry them off for burial. Their estimates of the dead range from 10,000 to 50,000, and that when the citizens of the town emerged at the end of the siege, they looked, not like living people, but more like the dead.

Exam-style question, Section B

Explain why civilians suffered during warfare, 1250–1500.

You may use the following in your answer:
- the Assize of Arms
- purveyance

You **must** also use information of your own. **12 marks**

Exam tip

This question tests understanding of features of the time and causation. Your answer should:
- include your **own information** to add to the points in the question
- focus constantly on the **reasons** for suffering
- give **evidence** or **examples** for all the reasons it gives.

A very good answer will give an **analysis** of the reasons. For example, it might point out that suffering was caused by a **combination** of reasons working together.

1.2 The experience of warfare

> **Activity**
>
> In groups, role-play a king and his barons planning a campaign in France in 1450. Decide:
>
> a What you need to fight the war.
>
> b How you should get the things you need.
>
> Write up the minutes of your meeting.

The benefits?

As we have seen, sieges, raids, plunder and ransom were normal parts of warfare at this time. This inevitably meant that the impact of wars on civilians was mainly bad. However, there were some benefits.

- Civilians who joined the army could benefit from good wages. In 1350, during the Hundred Years' War, a labourer in England earned about 2d per day (equivalent to about £3.50 today). A master craftsman earned 4d per day (£7). But a mounted archer earned 6d (£10.50). Soldiers might also be able to share ransom money and booty (valuable goods, stolen from the enemy). So, fighting offered a good income for some civilians.

- Other civilians made goods needed in wars, such as fortifications, weapons, armour, carts and soldiers' clothes. The Hundred Years' War was a time of prosperity in England's construction, weapons and textiles industries. Citizens benefited from good, secure wages in these industries.

These benefits did not outweigh the suffering that wars caused to civilians, but they should be noted in the overall impact of warfare.

Summary

The experience of warfare, 1250–1500

- Feudal service, Assize of Arms and payment continued as the ways of recruiting troops.
- The relative importance of these three methods changed during the period 1200–1500.
- Training of troops changed for the better, but remained quite poor despite improvements.
- Because there was so much warfare, provisioning methods had to change.
- Changes in purveyance of food and stores of weapons made armies better supplied.
- Weaknesses in supplies meant that armies continued to go short and resort to plunder.
- Civilians suffered from the impact of the cost of war, recruitment methods and fighting.

Checkpoint

Strengthen

S1 Can you give details of feudal service, arrays of arms and payment of troops in this period?

S2 Can you describe how the importance of these recruitment methods changed over time?

S3 Can you describe, in detail, how troops were trained and provisioned?

S4 Can you describe the impact on civilians of the cost of wars, recruitment and fighting?

If you are not confident about any of these questions, look up answers on pages 27–32 and record the answers for future reference.

Challenge

C1 Can you explain how the decline of the feudal system caused recruitment to change?

C2 Can you explain how **a combination of factors** caused recruitment to change?

C3 Can you explain why training and provisioning of troops changed?

C4 Can you explain why war had an impact on civilians, 1200–1500?

If you are not confident about any of these questions, form a group with other students, discuss the answers and then record your conclusions. Your teacher can give you some hints.

1.3 The Battle of Falkirk, 1298

> **Learning outcomes**
> - Understand the reasons for the outcome of the Battle of Falkirk.
> - Understand the roles of William Wallace and Edward I in the battle.

The Scottish uprising, 1297

In 1297, Scotland was under the control of the English king, Edward I. But, the Scots resented English control and an uprising began. By August, the Scottish leader, William Wallace, had summoned an army of 6,000 men and threatened the key strategic castle at Stirling.

Edward I was on campaign in France. The Earl of Surrey raised an army, also 6,000 strong, and confronted the Scots at the Battle of Stirling Bridge. Wallace's infantry, using pikes and organised in schiltrons, inflicted a crushing defeat on the English (see page 19).

Wallace didn't stop there. He led 3,000 men in a raid on northern England. Edward I was now faced with a full-blown revolt in Scotland.

January–April 1298 Early problems

Royal writs (commands) were issued summoning troops to Scotland using feudal service and the Assize of Arms. By February, 21,000 troops had gathered, commanded by the Earl of Surrey. This was an unusually large number. It shows that, in 1298, the traditional medieval methods of recruitment for English armies, though in decline, could still raise a large army.

However, winter campaigning was not normal or popular and feudal armies were only used to short periods of campaigning. As time went by, and the season for spring sowing in the fields approached, men began to drift back to their homes. By March, only 10,000 remained and, by April, it was 5,000. This is a good example of the problems kings faced when trying to fight wars with feudal troops.

This force re-captured the castles of Roxburgh and Berwick. But, Edward ordered that no campaign should start before he arrived. During the delay, even more troops left for home, until only 1,500 remained.

May–July 1298 Edward marches north

Edward's march north was typical of the period.

- His route hugged the east coast, so that he could be supplied with food by sea.
- Along the way, he paused to capture Scottish castles, at Dalhousie, Dirleton and Tantalion. This illustrates the importance of having castles as secure bases.
- The Scottish countryside was a wasteland. Wallace's men had destroyed any crops useful to Edward. The English added to the destruction, burning houses to punish the local population.
- Food became scarce. The supplies of Edward's slow-moving baggage train ran short and bad weather stopped ships landing food at Leith. At times, his men's only food was peas and beans from the fields. Morale sank and a bloody fight broke out amongst his troops, leaving 80 men dead. But, the crisis passed. Edward found food at the priory at Coldstream, where his men consumed 600 sheep. Eventually, Edward's good planning secured his food supply as supplies arrived by sea, but his campaign had almost collapsed due to a shortage of food.

22 July 1298 The armies assemble

By July 1298, both armies were manoeuvring for position near Falkirk.

- Wallace's strategy was to surprise Edward's larger army with a night attack. However, his plans were betrayed by two Scottish nobles. This was not the last time in this campaign that Wallace suffered because of a lack of loyalty from Scottish nobles.
- Wallace now had no alternative but to resort to a battle. He couldn't afford to let Edward strengthen the strategic castle at Stirling. He had to confront Edward. He headed south of Stirling to stand in the way of Edward's route north.

In the early hours of 22 July, apparently by accident, the two armies spotted each other, about a mile apart. Even though attack had proved disastrous to English forces the year before, Edward took the bold decision to commit his forces to an all-out attack.

1.3 The Battle of Falkirk, 1298

Wallace decided to face the English attack.

- He chose a position on hard ground on the side of a hill, with a marsh in front of him and his rear protected by woods. But his flanks had no protection.
- His infantry formed four schiltrons. The schiltrons were flanked by archers to provide protection against attack. His cavalry were formed up behind the right flank, protected by the schiltrons and archers, but in a position to strike at English cavalry and infantry (see Figure 1.5 for details).

The English army

At the time of the battle, Edward's army probably consisted of:

- 2,000 cavalry
- 12,000 infantry, including 5,000 longbow archers and 500 crossbowmen.

Half the cavalry were feudal troops. The other half were raised by Assize of Arms, with a minority of paid troops. There were 11 earls and 115 senior knights (bannerets) from the senior nobility amongst Edward's cavalry. Most of the archers were Welsh. Most of the crossbowmen were French mercenaries.

Some historians say that desertions may have reduced the infantry numbers to below 10,000.

The Scottish army

William Wallace's army probably consisted of:

- 500 cavalry
- 9,500 infantry, including 1,500 archers.

Wallace summoned his army using a system like the English Assize of Arms. Each area of Scotland had to send men from all classes. As in England, this was not always popular; Wallace erected gallows near his camp as a warning to potential deserters. But the system provided Wallace with a good mix of infantry, archers and cavalry. One persistent problem that Wallace had with his army was that he was not a member of the nobility. Scottish nobles resented taking orders from him. They supported him when things were going well; but any sign of problems and some were quick to desert him.

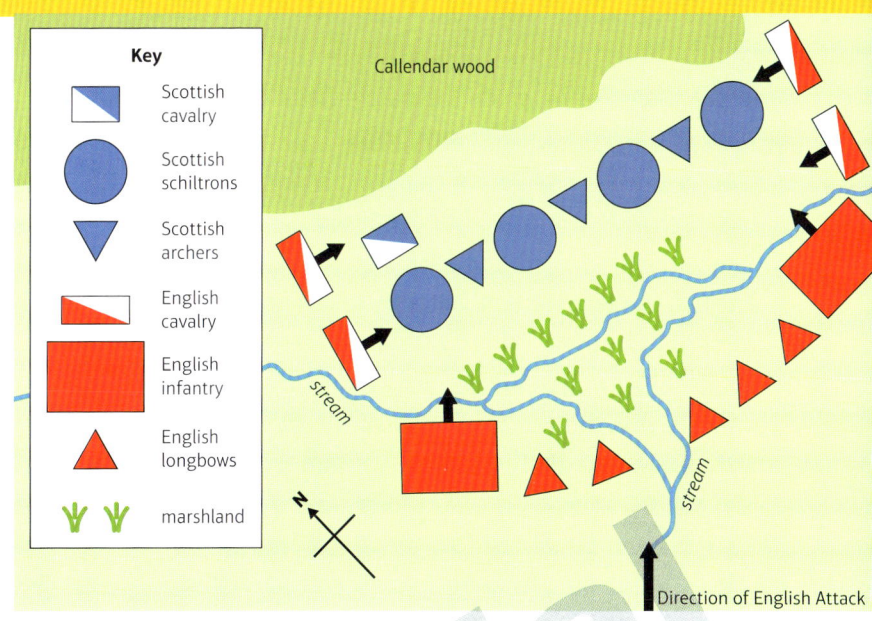

Figure 1.5 A plan of the Battle of Falkirk, 1298.

22 July 1298 The battle begins

As was normal, Edward consulted his earls in a council of war; he decided to launch a cavalry attack.

- At first, the **marsh** in front of the Scots slowed the attack. But, eventually, the English cavalry found ways around the marsh and confronted the Scottish flanks.
- An order was sent not to engage in combat before the king's cavalry group arrived. However, some of the feudal knights were too **undisciplined** to take orders.
- In some disorder, an uncoordinated cavalry attack began. Fortunately for the English, it achieved two important successes. First, they forced the **Scottish cavalry** off the field. The English cavalry outnumbered the Scots by four to one; so this is not surprising. However, the Scottish cavalry seem to have abandoned the battlefield with little resistance, showing little loyalty to Wallace. Second, free from their foe, the English cavalry charged into the gaps between the **Scottish archers** and the schiltrons. This completely cut off the Scottish archers, and the English cavalry was able to charge in amongst them, killing or driving off the majority.
- Edward's attack then ran into problems. The English cavalry turned to attack the **schiltrons**, but they had no success whatsoever. The solid rows of pikes stood firm. This was very unusual; cavalry were used to charging through infantry lines. But Wallace's schiltrons were well disciplined and the English cavalry could not penetrate their solid lines of pikes. The English attack stalled.

33

1.3 The Battle of Falkirk, 1298

This was the point at which the battle was decided. Edward deployed his 5,000 **longbows**.

- Clouds of arrows fell upon the Scottish infantry. Unprotected by armour, hundreds died.
- Gaps appeared in the walls of Scottish pikes and the **English cavalry** were at last able to charge into the weak spots. Soon, Wallace's troops scattered.
- Finally, the **English infantry** attacked. Any Scottish infantry who did not reach the safety of the woods were hacked to death by English infantry or chased and killed by the mounted cavalry.

Edward had won the battle. He set about capturing **castles** and taking a firmer grip on Scotland. Wallace escaped, but was later captured. He was taken to London, where he was executed.

The role of William Wallace

Wallace's decisions played a key part in the battle – and thus in the future history of Scotland.

- Wallace's use of pike **schiltrons** nearly worked. Even after their cavalry protection had been driven off and their archers had been destroyed, they beat off the first cavalry attack against them.
- Aspects of Wallace's choice of **position** – the slope, the marsh, the woods – were good.
- He failed to protect his **flanks**: a basic command error.
- Wallace's **cavalry** and his **archers** played no useful part in the battle. Some would say that this was his fault for choosing to face the enemy with inadequate troops. However, this was the first battle where English archers showed their strength.

In the end, his choice to stand and fight cost him his life and his country's freedom.

The role of Edward I

Edward I nearly lost this campaign.

- Despite detailed plans to supply his troops by sea, they were nearly defeated by **hunger**. His advanced planning was admirable; but it only just worked.
- Despite having superior forces, **undisciplined cavalry** could have ruined his attack. Against a stronger enemy, it could have been disastrous. Edward was lucky.
- However, by his bold decision to attack, Edward had forced Wallace to fight in a position where his flanks were undefended. In battles at this time, outmanoeuvring your enemy (moving your forces around so that you get a better position than your enemy) was a key skill for commanders.
- Edward's use of his **longbows** was the turning point of the battle. It became a key part of English strategy in warfare for the next 150 years.

Edward overcame difficulties and then made the most of his superior troops.

Activities

1. In groups of four, take it in turns to name features of the Battle of Falkirk that were **typical** of battles, 1250–1500. Jot down each correct idea.
2. Split the class in two, Scots and English. Debate: 'Why did the English win the Battle of Falkirk?' Consider the number and composition of troops, tactics used, the role of individual commanders. At the end, record the best points made.
3. 'The Battle of Falkirk was a victory of infantry over cavalry.' Decide whether you agree and then write a paragraph to explain your view.

Summary

- Features of Wallace's rebellion, Edward's campaign and their battle at Falkirk were **typical** of warfare at this time.
- The Scottish schiltrons showed that pikes could make infantry very effective against cavalry. This was part of the slow decline of cavalry as the dominant force on the battlefield.
- The English archers showed the dominance on the battlefield that they were to display for the next 150 years.

Checkpoint

Challenge

C1 Can you give details to justify each of the three statements made in the Summary above?

If you are not sure, go back to the text in this section to find the details you need.

1.4 The Battle of Agincourt, 1415

> **Learning outcomes**
> - Understand the reasons for the outcome of the Battle of Agincourt.
> - Understand the role of Henry V in the battle.

During the Hundred Years' War, Henry V of England tried to conquer land in Northern France.

Recruitment

Henry's army was raised by paying for **indentures** (contracts) with noblemen willing to act as **captains** of bodies of troops for 12 months. For example:

- The Duke of Clarence, the king's brother, supplied 720 men-at-arms and 240 archers.
- The Duke of York, the king's cousin, supplied 100 men-at-arms and 300 archers.

These were the same type of men who, 200 years earlier, would have supplied feudal troops. To reduce the cost, Henry agreed that troops capturing **booty** on the campaign could keep a third of its value, a third would be taken by the captains and a third given to the Crown.

Henry's invasion force

The army used ships **hired** from Holland or **impressed** (taken, by royal order) from private owners in England.

- Henry had 12,000 troops, 9,000 of whom were archers.
- The indentures show a ratio of 1:3 – one mounted **man-at-arms** to three mounted **archers**.

Henry's strategy

Henry's declared aim was to **capture** and **control** land in northern France. But, the composition of his army shows that he did not intend to do this by defeating the French army in **battle**. He had too few men-at-arms to fight offensive battles.

Instead, he planned to seize French **castles** and **raid** French settlements with his fast-moving army, destroying property and seizing booty. He then planned to negotiate with the French king for territory.

So, having landed in France in August 1415, Henry spent five weeks seizing the port of **Harfleur**. In early October, leaving troops to protect the town, Henry set out for the English stronghold at Calais, to take refuge for the winter.

Henry's march across France

Even though it became a journey of 250 miles across enemy territory, Henry chose to **march** to Calais, rather than **sail**, to show the French he was not scared of them.

- The French had gathered a large army, led by Charles d'Albret, to confront Henry. They shadowed Henry's movements, trying to force him into a battle.
- **Dysentery** – a disease known at the time as 'the bloody flux' – had already broken out amongst Henry's men in Harfleur. The Earl of Sussex and many others had died of it. As Henry's march stretched into its third week, in wintry weather, his men became increasingly ill, weak and tired.
- The French doggedly kept themselves between Henry's army and his route to Calais. Eventually, they trapped the English and Henry was forced to accept battle.

Henry's army

Henry probably had 8,000 troops at Agincourt, of whom 2,000 were men-at-arms and 6,000 archers.

The French army

Probably 15,000 troops, of whom 10,000 were heavily armoured cavalry and only 5,000 were infantry. French archers were available, but were hardly used.

> **Source A**
>
> An image from a French chronicle (c1400) showing English troops besieging a town.

35

1.4 The Battle of Agincourt, 1415

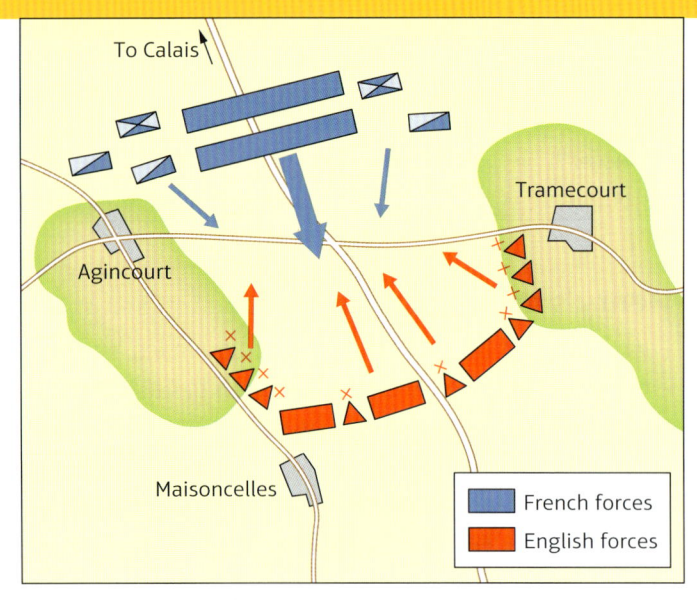

Figure 1.6 A plan of the Battle of Agincourt, 1415.

The armies take up positions

Henry did not choose the location of the battle.

- But, he sent knights to survey the land the night before, then placed his army in a narrow gap, 750 metres wide, between two **woods**. There was **ploughed land** between him and the French army. It was wet, heavy clay, which Henry knew that the French would find difficult to cross. The French knights made it worse, by exercising horses there, churning up the mud.
- The English men-at-arms dismounted and made a **defensive** block in the centre of the army.
- The archers were placed on the two **flanks**. Henry ordered archers to hammer angled **stakes** into the ground in front of his troops to slow the enemy cavalry attack.

Meanwhile, the French army assembled, some 1,000 metres away.

25 October 1415 Battle begins

Henry took the initiative. He sent archers into the trees to fire at the French lines. This was called **galling**; the French knights regarded it as unchivalrous. Their code of chivalry was for a 'fair' contest, knight against knight, in the open. Angry, they lost their discipline and began a disorganised charge. The infantry moved up behind them.

It was at this point that the English longbows showed their value.

- **Longbow** archers fired in volleys into the flanks or directly onto the heads of the French cavalry.
- **Wounded horses**, slowed by heavy rain-soaked clay, fell or panicked, crashing into others. The charge failed and the French **cavalry** retreated – directly into the approaching French infantry.
- The French **infantry** arrived at the battlefront, exhausted, having slogged through mud over the bodies of fallen men. The narrow battlefront made their numeric advantage useless (see Source B).
- Henry then **attacked**. His archers put down their bows and attacked from the flanks with swords. The English men-at-arms pressed forward. The French, crowded together and stumbling on bodies, retreated.

Source B

The contemporary French chronicler, the monk of St Denis, was not present at the battle, but lived at the time and wrote a six volume history of France around the time of the Battle of Agincourt.

Marching through the middle of the mud... they sank up to their knees. So they were already overcome with fatigue even before they advanced against the enemy... The first wave of about 5,000 men was so tightly packed that the third rank could not use their swords.

The battle had lasted only about three hours, yet it was a significant victory.

- Estimates vary, but it is thought that about 450 English died. Henry's victory saved the English army from destruction and avoided the capture or death of the English king.
- For France, it was much worse. Again, estimates vary, but it was widely thought at the time that 4,000 Frenchmen died. These included their commander, three dukes, five counts and 90 barons. This was a significant number of the French ruling class. 1,500 noblemen were also taken prisoner.
- In military terms, the Battle of Agincourt became a prime example of the dominance of the **longbow**, but Henry's sieges, like the one at Harfleur, were important too. It was the control of fortified bases that gave Henry **military** and **political control** of the surrounding countryside.

1.4 The Battle of Agincourt, 1415

Source C

A painting of the Battle of Agincourt. It is a copy, made in 1900, of a painting in a medieval manuscript. The scenery is fanciful and showing the English cavalry (on the right) charging is wrong. But the ploughed ground, weapons, protective clothing and chaos amongst French troops are correct.

Interpretation 1

Description of the French army from *The Art of War in the Middle Ages, AD378–1515*, by historian C. Oman (1885).

[The French army] was composed of a fiery and undisciplined aristocracy that imagined itself to be the most efficient military force in the world, but was in reality little removed from an armed mob.

Reasons for the outcome

- **Positioning the armies.** Henry chose an ideal defensive position.
- **French tactics.** The French relied too much on cavalry. Their infantry and archers were weak and underused by the French commanders.
- **French indiscipline**. Their cavalry attack was badly co-ordinated with the infantry.
- **The longbow.** The English could fire up to 100,000 arrows per minute at the French attack.

The role of Henry V

In some ways, Henry was fortunate to win.

- His march across France was risky and it weakened his army.
- He was outmanoeuvred and forced to fight a battle that he wanted to avoid.

But he showed key skills as a commander by his:

- choice of a good defensive position
- placement of men-at-arms and archers
- use of longbows as the decisive force.

Henry also showed a key quality of medieval commanders – bravery and the ability to fight on the battlefield as an example to his men. Several of the contemporary sources describe Henry fighting side-by-side with his men-at-arms, scattering the enemy with his axe, even when his crown, worn in the battle over his helmet, was split by a blow from a French axe.

1.4 The Battle of Agincourt, 1415

> ### Activities
> 1. Draw a timeline of the Battle of Agincourt, recording the key events from the positioning of armies to the final victory of the English in the final mêlée.
> 2. Make a table to show features of the Agincourt campaign that were **typical** of the time. Use, as rows in your table, 'Recruitment', 'Size and Composition of Army', 'Strategy and Tactics', 'Battle'.
> 3. Consider this statement: 'Henry V was the main reason the English won the Battle of Agincourt.' One half of the class should write paragraphs in favour, one half against. Decide which point of view is the most persuasive. Record your decision and reasons.

THINKING HISTORICALLY — Change and continuity (2b)

Events or historical change?

Change is an alteration in a situation. Events are when something happens.

Sometimes a situation can be very different before and after an event – this event **marks a change**. However, sometimes a situation is the same before and after an event, and sometimes a situation changes without a specific event taking place at all.

Study the following events and their changes::

The Battle of Stirling Bridge (1297)	The English army become more successful, especially against French knights.	English civilians suffered from higher taxation and unfair requisitioning of goods.	The introduction of the longbow into English armies at the Battle of Falkirk (1298)
The Hundred Years' War (1337–1453)	More Englishmen are forced to fight in the king's army.	An increase in the use of pikes to defend against cavalry and even attack infantry.	The Statute of Winchester (1285)

1. Sort the above into 'events' and 'changes'.
2. Match each event to the change that it marks.
3. Can you think of an historical change that has happened without there being a particular event associated with it? An example would be the decline of feudalism in the 14th century.
4. What is the difference between an event and a change?

Summary

- Several features of the Battle of Agincourt, such as the recruitment and composition of the armies, were typical of warfare at this time.
- The English victory demonstrated the key role of the longbow in warfare during this period.
- The decisions of the English and French commanders illustrate some of the key strategies and tactics of warfare during this period.

Checkpoint

Challenge

C1 Can you give details to justify each of the three statements made in the Summary above?

If you are not sure, go back to the text in this section to find the details you need.

Re-cap c1250-c1500: Warfare and English society

Draw a table showing continuity and change in Warfare c1250-c1500 based on the one below. Draw larger coloured boxes and use these to note down evidence for each of the examples of Continuity, Change, Trend / Turning Point, Factors and Consequences in the table. The evidence will be detailed information like statistics, a key battle, a new law, etc.

Change and continuity	Patterns of change	Factors affecting warfare
Continuity	**Trend or turning point**	**Factor affecting change**
Size of armies	**Turning point** — Improved use of pikes and schiltrons	Society
Command of armies		Science
Limited warfare	**Turning point** — Increased use of longbows	Technology
Importance of castles		
Importance of positioning		
Change	**Trend** — Increasing use of gunpowder weapons	**Consequence on civilians**
Power of pikes		Increased taxation
Use of longbows		Requisition of food
Changes in armour		Requisition of goods
Composition of armies	**Trend** — Decline of the mounted knight	Impact of recruitment
New tactics		Impact of fighting
Gunpowder weapons		Benefits of recruitment
Decline of mounted knight	**Trend** — Decline of the feudal system	Other benefits of warfare
Changes in recruitment		
Changes in training		
Changes in provisioning		

The Battle of Bosworth, 1485

Read through these features and have a go at the activities on the right.

- The battle was fought by **small armies**. Richard III had 12,000 men; Henry Tudor 5,000.
- Both armies consisted of **infantry** and **cavalry**.
- Richard's army contained levies from shires and towns, raised by **Assize of Arms**, and **paid** troops. Henry's army, raised abroad, consisted entirely of paid **mercenaries**.
- In the early stages, Richard's army was weakened by **arrows** from Henry's archers.
- Richard **positioned** himself on a hill; this weakened the impact of Henry's cavalry.
- Richard's army contained a number of **cannon** – sources suggest as many as 140.
- Richard's key tactic was a **cavalry charge**, intended to capture Henry.
- Richard was eventually killed, probably by halberds and swords, in **hand-to-hand** combat.
- Many of Richard's army were killed as they **fled**, chased by Henry's cavalry.

Activities

1. This section has covered the period 1250–1500. The Battle of Falkirk (1298) illustrates warfare in about 1250. For comparison, listed left are the features of the Battle of Bosworth (1485), which illustrate the key features of warfare in 1500. Add the Battle of Bosworth to the table that you started on page 26.

2. In a group, think about this interpretation from a modern military historian: 'This was a period of change caused, not merely by technical factors, but also by social, political and economic realities.' Write a list of changes in warfare 1250–1500 that are evidence to support this interpretation.

WRITING HISTORICALLY

Writing historically: a clear response

Every response you write needs to be clearly written. To help you achieve this, you need to clearly signal that your response is relevant to the question you are answering.

Learning outcomes

By the end of this lesson, you will understand how to:
- use key noun phrases from the question to make sure you are answering it
- use the subject-verb construction to clearly express an idea or opinion.

Definitions

Noun: a word that names an object, idea, person, place, etc (for example, 'William', 'king', 'castle')

Noun phrase: a phrase including a noun and any words that modify its meaning, (for example, 'the king of England', 'a motte and bailey castle'.)

Verb: words that describe actions ('William conquered England'), incidents ('The battle ended') and situations ('William was king for 21 years')

How can I make sure I am answering the question?

Look at this exam-style question in which key noun phrases and verbs are highlighted:

> Explain why English armies stopped using the longbow between the Battle of Bosworth (1485) and 1600.

Now look at the first two sentences from two different responses to this question below.

Answer A

> Although the English had won the Battle of Agincourt with the longbow, use began to decline from 1485 and by 1600 it had disappeared from English armies. English armies adopted the musket instead.

Answer B

> English armies adopted the musket. These were gunpowder firearms that fired lead balls.

1. a. Which answer signals most clearly that their response is going to answer the question?
   b. Write a sentence or two explaining your choice.

2. Now look at this exam-style question:

   > Explain **one** way in which the composition of the army was different in the early 17th and early 19th centuries.

3. Which are the key noun phrases and verbs in this question? Note them down.
   b. Write the first two sentences of your response to this question.
   c. Look again at the first two sentences of your response. Highlight all the key noun phrases and verbs from the question that you have included in your sentences. Have you used them all? If not, try re-writing your sentences, including them all to clearly signal that your response is answering the question.

WRITING HISTORICALLY

How can I clearly express my ideas?

One way to introduce your opinions and ideas clearly and briefly is by using a short statement sentence beginning with a **subject-verb** construction.

English armies introduced the musket. The musket was more powerful than the longbow.

This is the main verb in this sentence. It tells you what English armies did.

This noun is the subject of the main verb. It tells you it was English armies that did it.

This is the main verb in this sentence. It tells you about the situation.

This noun is the subject of the main verb. It tells you who or what the verb refers to.

4. Look again at Answer A's opening sentences:

Although the English had won the Battle of Agincourt with the longbow, use began to decline from 1485 and by 1600 it had disappeared from English armies. English armies adopted the musket instead.

This short statement expresses the writer's approach to the question clearly and briefly.

This is the main verb in this sentence. This noun phrase is the subject of the sentence.

The writer could have written:

English armies adopted the musket instead of the longbow by 1600, despite the fact that they had won the Battle of Agincourt with it.

Or

Even though the English had won the Battle of Agincourt, their armies adopted the musket instead of the longbow by 1600.

Which version do you prefer? Write a sentence or two explaining your choice.

5. a. Try re-writing the same information using different sentence structures to all the versions above.
   b. Is your version clearer or more succinct than Answer A's sentences?

Improving an answer

Look at this exam question:

> Explain **one** way in which the composition of the army was different in the early 17th and early 19th centuries.

Now look at one response to it:

In 1600, there was a combination of pikemen and musketeers. In 1800, they were no longer divided into musketeers and pikemen – the invention of the bayonet meant that they just had soldiers with muskets or rifles, and bayonets.

6. Re-write the response so that:
   a. the opening sentences focus on key words and phrases from the question
   b. it includes a short statement sentence beginning with a subject-verb construction to clearly introduce the writer's approach to the question.

41

Preparing for your exams

Each book has a section dedicated to explaining and exemplifying the new Edexcel GCSE (9–1) History exams. Advice on the demands of every paper, written by **Angela Leonard**, suggests ways students can successfully approach each exam. Each question type is then explained through annotated sample answers at two levels, showing clearly how answers can be improved.

Preparing for your exams

Preparing for your GCSE Paper 1 exam

Paper 1 overview

Your Paper 1 is in two sections that examine the Historic Environment and the Thematic Study. Together they count for 30% of your History assessment. The questions on the Thematic Study: Warfare through time are in Section B and are worth 20% of your History assessment. Allow two-thirds of the examination time for Section B. There are an extra four marks for the assessment of Spelling, Punctuation and Grammar in the last question.

History Paper 1	Historic Environment and Thematic Depth Study			Time 1 hour 15 mins
Section A	Historic Environment	Answer 3 questions	16 marks	25 mins
Section B	Thematic Study	Answer 3 questions	32 marks + 4 SPaG marks	50 mins

Warfare and British society, c1250–present

You will answer Questions 3 and 4, and then **either** Question 5 or Question 6.

Q3 Explain one way… (4 marks)

You are given about half a page of lines to write about a similarity or a difference. Allow five minutes to write your answer.
This question is only worth four marks and you should keep the answer brief. Only one comparison is needed. You should compare by referring to both periods given in the question – for example, '*xxx was similar because in the Middle Ages… and also in the 16th century…*'

Q4 Explain why… (12 marks)

This question asks you to explain the reasons why something happened. Allow about 15 minutes to write your answer.
You are given two information points as prompts to help you. You do not have to use the prompts and you will not lose marks by leaving them out. Higher marks are gained by adding in a point extra to the prompts. You will be given at least two pages of lines in the answer booklet for your answer. This does not mean you should try to fill all the space. Aim to write an answer giving at least three explained reasons.

EITHER 5 OR 6 How far do you agree? (16 marks +4 for SPaG)

This question, including SPaG, is worth 20 marks – more than half your marks for the whole of the Thematic Study. Make sure you have kept 30 minutes of the exam time to answer it and to check your spelling, punctuation and grammar.

You have a choice: 5 or 6. Before you decide, be clear what each statement in the questions is about and what topic information you will need to answer it. You will have prompts to help, as for Question 4.

The statement can be about the concepts of: cause, significance, consequence, change, continuity, similarity, difference. It is a good idea during revision to practise identifying the concept focus of statements. For example, the statement "Mounted knights declined because of the longbow", is a statement about cause.

You must make a judgment on **how far you agree** and you should think about **both** sides of the argument. Plan your answer before you begin to write, putting your answer points in two columns: For and Against. You should consider at least three points. Think about it as if you were putting weight on each side to decide what your judgment is going to be for the conclusion. That way your whole answer hangs together – it is coherent.

Be clear about your reasons (your criteria) for your judgment – for example, why one cause is more important than another. Did it perhaps set others in motion? You must **explain** your answer.

In this question, four extra marks will be gained for good Spelling, Punctuation and Grammar. Use sentences, paragraphs, capital letters, commas and full stops, etc. Try also to use specialist terms specific to your Thematic Study – for example, feudal duty, scutage, schiltrons, etc.

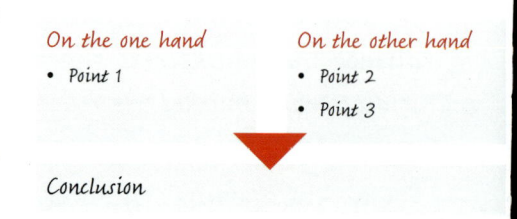

On the one hand
- Point 1

On the other hand
- Point 2
- Point 3

Conclusion

Preparing for your exams

Paper 1, Questions 3 & 4

Question 3. Explain **one** way in which the composition of the army was different in the early 17th and early 19th centuries. **(4 marks)**

Average answer

In 1600 they had pikemen and musketeers in the infantry but in 1800 they didn't.

Verdict

This is an average answer because the difference is not explained.

Question 4. Explain why English armies stopped using the longbow between the Battle of Bosworth (1485) and 1600.
You may use the following in your answer:
- developments in armour
- changes in society

You **must** also use information of your own. **(12 marks)**

Average answer

English armies stopped using the longbow and started using the musket after new armour was invented at the end of the sixteenth century that used high carbon steel. This was much stronger than the old armour, and it was almost arrow proof.

Changes in society meant there were not so many men who could use a longbow because they didn't have time to practise.

The guns got better as well. The new matchlock musket was much quicker to reload than the old ones and it could fire every two minutes. It was so heavy that it still needed a rest to support the end though.

Information is accurate but too descriptive. There is some development, but not directly linked to the question.

This is a valid reason, but needs to be supported with specific information.

Relevant extra information in addition to the stimulus points. But, it isn't used to answer the question.

Verdict

This is an average answer because:
- information is accurate, showing some knowledge and understanding of the period and adds a point beyond the stimulus material (so it is not a weak answer)
- it does not analyse causes explicitly enough to be a strong answer – it should be much more specific about answering the **why** in the question
- there is some development of factual material, but the line of reasoning is not clear.

Use the feedback to rewrite these answers, making as many improvements as you can.

Preparing for your exams

Each book has a section dedicated to explaining and exemplifying the new Edexcel GCSE (9–1) History exams. Advice on the demands of every paper, written by **Angela Leonard**, suggests ways students can successfully approach each exam. Each question type is then explained through annotated sample answers at two levels, showing clearly how answers can be improved.

Preparing for your exams

Paper 2, Question 1

Explain **two** consequences of the decisions made by the Grand Alliance at the Yalta Conference in February 1945. **(8 marks)**

> **Exam tip**
>
> The question wants you to explain the results of something. What difference did it make? Use phrases such as 'as a result' or 'the effect of this was'.

Strong answer

Consequence 1:

At the Yalta Conference the Big Three decided what would happen to Germany after the war. As a result of the conference Germany was divided into four zones, controlled by Britain, the USA, the Soviet Union and France. Each country had the right to govern its sector as it saw fit. However, Stalin believed that in the end he had been given the poorest sector and resented the fact that the Western Allies administered the wealthier parts. So this led to worse relations between East and West as Germany became an area of tension.

A clear explanation of the impact of the division of Germany, with specific factual support.

Consequence 2:

Yalta led to an increase in suspicion between Stalin and the USA/Britain. This suspicion was as a result of the failure to agree on how Poland should be governed. There was general agreement that a government would be elected using free elections, but this meant different things to each country. To Stalin it meant using his influence to ensure a pro-Moscow government. Britain and the USA supported the 'London Poles' who were non-communists. Stalin wanted a communist government in Poland as part of his plan to build a buffer zone. He saw the action of Britain and the USA as trying to undermine the security of the Soviet Union. So relations worsened.

A valid point very well explained, with a high level of factual support.

Verdict

This is a strong answer because it has explained two consequences and supported both with specific information showing good knowledge of the period.

The Student Books are only one element of our resources offering...

ActiveLearn
Digital Service

Check out what's available online too!

→

Like what you see in the Student Books?
There's even more available online...

We've created a whole host of time-saving digital tools and materials to help you plan, teach, track and assess the new Edexcel GCSE (9–1) qualification with confidence.

ActiveLearn
Digital Service

- **Editable lesson plans you can tailor to your students**
  - ✓ Linked to the Edexcel schemes of work
  - ✓ Filled with differentiation ideas to engage all your students with history

- **Online Student Books (ActiveBooks) to use with your classes**
  - ✓ Include zoomable sources, images and activities, perfect for front-of-class teaching
  - ✓ Embedded teaching and learning resources to inspire your lessons, such as video introductions and source materials for the Historic Environment unit

- **Ready-made student worksheets**
  - ✓ Designed to complement the Student Books and lesson plans
  - ✓ Editable, so you can personalise them to your students' needs

- **Extra materials for Thinking Historically and Writing Historically**
  - ✓ Teacher notes to help you use the Student Books' *Thinking Historically* and *Writing Historically* pedagogies with your classes
  - ✓ Additional worksheets to support your students as they develop their conceptual understanding and historical literacy skills

- **Assessment materials to help your students get set for the new exams**
  - ✓ Exam skills PowerPoints with exam questions and sample answers
  - ✓ Realistic exam-style assessments and mark schemes for each unit – ideal for exam practice
  - ✓ Diagnostic assessments linked to the Pearson Progression Scale to help you and your students pinpoint strengths and weaknesses

Sign up to hear more at **www.pe**